THE
OFF-ISLANDER

THE
OFF-ISLANDER

Peter Colt

KENSINGTON BOOKS
www.kensingtonbooks.com

KENSINGTON BOOKS are published by

Kensington Publishing Corp.
119 West 40th Street
New York, NY 10018

All Kensington titles, imprints, and distributed lines are available at special quantity discounts for bulk purchases for sales promotion, premiums, fund-raising, educational, or institutional use.

Special book excerpts or customized printings can also be created to fit specific needs. For details, write or phone the office of the Kensington Special Sales Manager: Attn.: Special Sales Department. Kensington Publishing Corp, 119 West 40th Street, New York, NY 10018. Phone: 1-800-221-2647.

Kensington and the K logo Reg. U.S. Pat. & TM Off.

Library of Congress Card Catalogue Number: 2019940168

ISBN-13: 978-1-4967-2341-3
ISBN-10: 1-4967-2341-4
First Kensington Hardcover Edition: October 2019

ISBN-13: 978-1-4967-2345-1 (ebook)
ISBN-10: 1-4967-2345-7 (ebook)

10 9 8 7 6 5 4 3 2 1

Printed in the United States of America

For Cathy, Henry and Alder

And for my father, he would have liked this.

Acknowledgments

It is simple to think that a writer writes a book and a publisher publishes it, but in reality, there is much more to it; there are loads of people who make the book a tangible thing. I will not be able to thank everyone who helped this book leave my computer and find its way into the hands of the reader. Any omission is one of oversight and not a slight.

The author wishes to thank the following people without whom this never would have happened: My agent Cynthia Manson who offered advice, support and most importantly worked very hard to find the book a home. John Scognamiglio at Kensington who liked it enough to champion it. CME who cleaned up the drafts, no small feat; and the many friends and family who read the manuscript and offered advice and encouragement. My wife Cathy without whom this could never have happened.

Prologue

"No shit, there I was . . ." All good war stories began that way. FWAP. A bullet smashed into the wood above my head. Then the crack of the rifle. I had heard it before, but I never quite got used to being shot at. The sound of the bullet as it whizzes by you and then impacts on something.

No shit, there I was. I shouldn't have been there. I got home after three years of fighting in Vietnam and I was never going to get shot at again. That was what I told myself. FWAP. Another fucking bullet. I'd promised myself!

I glanced over at her. The girl was next to me. She wasn't bleeding and seemed unhurt. That was good. I had dragged her into this, and I didn't want to see anything bad happen to her. FWAP. He was a persistent fucker, and I was a stupid one.

I wasn't going to be shot at again. That was the plan leaving Vietnam. Part of my not being shot at again plan had been going back to college. Somehow, in my head, the college-educated get shot at less than guys like me from South Boston, Southie. Then I left college. I became a cop.

I fucked that plan up again. For five years, almost six, I was a cop in Boston.

In the army the people trying to kill me were hard-core professional killers, Viet Cong, North Vietnamese Army, they were good. Elite. In the cops, everyone was trying to kill me. Either it was criminals with varying degrees of skill, or random shit like car accidents, or other cops just doing stupid shit, or the most dangerous of all—amateurs who just got lucky.

The cops was dangerous, Vietnam had been dangerous . . . but there had been an order to the chaos. There was a beautiful symmetry to Vietnam. Yes, death could be random or accidental, but usually it wasn't. In the cops it was so random, so chaotic that it made no sense at all. Then I quit. I vowed that no one was ever going to shoot at me again.

Now I was lying facedown on wet grass. I was wondering how what seemed like a simple missing person case had turned into something where people were shooting at me again. This wasn't supposed to happen anymore . . . that was the plan. I wasn't a tough guy. I was supposed to spend my days working a little and my nights drinking and trying to bed women. That was the plan.

Oh well, to hell with the plan.

Chapter 1

Danny Sullivan had a wedge-shaped face, narrow, pointy chin, and a brain that put to shame anything made by IBM. He wore a beard and mustache that were thin and neatly groomed. Danny's red hair, pale, freckled skin, and green eyes left no doubt that he was more Irish than the leprechaun on Notre Dame's uniforms. His suit came from Brooks Brothers, a lightweight summer one in a shade of tan that reminded me too much of the army. It was well tailored and spoke of Danny's unstoppable upward mobility.

Danny is my oldest and closest friend. It has been that way since kindergarten. We ran track together in high school. He stayed the course, went to Harvard Law, and later went on to protest the war with legal opinions and pro bono work for anyone against it. I swerved in the other direction. I quit school and found myself in a recruiter's office, then in the army. Danny traded defending war protestors for free for defending real criminals for real money. I traded textbooks for a free membership to the local VA hospital, marred skin, and dreams I don't like to talk about. Danny eventually became a respectable Republican and was working his way deeper into the upper crust. In keeping with being raised in South Boston, Southie, we referred to each other as Andy and Danny, not Dan or Daniel, and certainly never Andrew. It was a Southie sign of familiarity. Michael was a saint, Mikey was your friend. Nicholas was the name your parents used when you got in trouble, later when you were in court. To your close friends, you were Nicky. It was our only concession to the old neighborhood.

"Andy." He pointed a finger at me like it was a pistol; the other three fingers were wrapped around a glass of scotch with a name I couldn't pronounce and price I could only afford when a relative died. "Andy, the client wants an investigator, one that can keep his mouth shut and is willing to break a rule or two." Danny was all class. Now he said things like investigator instead of private eye. I knew him before there was a gas tank with HO CHI MINH painted on it casting shadows over the old neighborhood. These days, Danny acts as though he has to look out for me. He feels guilty that I went to Nam and he didn't. He is annoyed because I haven't had much interest in trying to catch the middle-class brass ring—a stable job, a wife, kids, house, a mortgage, and a dog. I have tried to explain to him, but he just thinks that I am using Vietnam as an excuse to be a fuckup.

I lifted the pilsner glass of Löwenbräu to my lips and listened to his sales pitch. I didn't need much of one. I was between jobs and had time to spare. I don't do well with too much time off. My apartment seems too big, too dusty, and too empty these days. The Karmann Ghia was going to need a new clutch soon, and I had known Danny long enough that when he wanted me to take a job for a client, I took it.

"Andy, she is a little idiosyncratic—she wants you to fly

out to San Francisco to meet with her. Fly out on her nickel and hear what she has to say."

"Why doesn't she come out here if the case is here?" Usually clients come to the investigator; it is what makes all those detective novels so interesting in the beginning. The leggy brunette with a husky voice and trouble written all over her walking through a frosted-glass-paneled door.

"Andy, she is rich and she has commitments, and you like San Francisco. Go out there, hear what she has to say, see if you can help her. Have a nice meal, stay in a nice hotel, and go out to Alcatraz, play at being a tourist, maybe meet a nice lady for a night . . ." He trailed off at that.

"I haven't been back to San Francisco in years." I remember getting off of the chartered Pan Am flight, walking up the Jetway and into the airport. People stared at my uniform, stared at me. No one spat on me or anything dramatic. I just knew that I was in a strange, unwelcoming land. In the bars, my tan and my short hair gave me away, and there were a lot of ladies who didn't want anything to do with me. I remember a dark bar, someone saying "Baby Killer," and a fight. I remember the feel of a nose giving way under my fist, a leg giving way to a knee in someone's crotch, and the cop's nightstick against my head. I never held any of it against the city.

"Yes, man, that is it. Go hear her out and take the case." Danny was pressing hard.

"Important client?" He wore glasses, and the light played off of them, making it hard to see his eyes.

"A rich client, whose rich husband has a bright political future." Danny had given up liberalism and the antiwar movement to drive a Cadillac to work and have a Mercedes in the garage for the wife. Danny's wife had the type of ambition that had dragged them out of Southie. It would have made Danny's very Catholic mother angry, except for the fact that the Protestant wife was a Republican and the mother of their two daughters, who are already going to the right schools in first grade.

"Political future in California? I thought that was for Democrats only?"

"Look at Reagan. Andy, people aren't stupid anymore. They gave up on peanut farmers who can't get them gas for their cars or keep the mullahs in check. I am telling you, California . . . well, maybe not LA, but California is going to be the next Republican state." Ronald Reagan had beaten Carter, and we were a couple of years into his first term. I liked his hair—that was about all I could say.

"Okay, call her and tell her I will make arrangements to fly out." I raised the pilsner glass to my lips, and when I looked back at him, Danny was grinning the grin that prosecuting attorneys had come to hate. He reached down and swung his briefcase up onto the table with the same ease that Bjorn Borg served. I listened to the double snap of the catches opening and lost sight of his face when the lid went up. A Pan Am ticket envelope landed in front of me next to my empty glass.

"She wants to meet you tonight. I booked you on the 2:15 from Logan."

I picked up the envelope and held it pinched between my fingers.

"You knew I would say yes."

Danny smiled that smile that reminded me of sharks and wolves. "I knew you would. You have never let me down before." The way he said it I wondered how much this client meant to him. I slid the envelope in the pocket of my corduroy sport coat.

"I guess I should run, then." I stood and we shook hands. I made my way through the restaurant to the street. The Ghia was where I left it. It was hunter green with a tan interior. I bought it used, a couple of years old from a coed in Cambridge whose father bought it for her new the last year they made them. She wanted to follow the Grateful Dead around. I wanted a car. I just loved the look of the car. I got in the Ghia and fought my way through lunchtime traffic to my apartment. I was living in a part of Back Bay that was nice but still affordable. I parked and hustled up the back stairs.

The apartment was a fourth floor one-bedroom that was hot in summer and cold in winter, but it did have a view of the Charles River. The building wasn't in the best shape, but you couldn't beat the location or the view. The door opened, and I walked into half an apartment. The bookshelves looked as though they had been ransacked by a burglar who specialized in fiction. I did have a TV, a small color one that I could watch the Red Sox on, but it wasn't good for much else.

In the bedroom, I had a bed but no bureau, a mirror but no bedside table. This was how my furniture looked after Leslie. It had been almost two months. I was still finding her hair stuck to my clothes and had just gotten past the point where the phone was in my hand and I had almost dialed her number.

In the closet, I found a canvas mailman's bag that I used as luggage. Into it went my shaving kit, a white button-down shirt, T-shirts, and everything else for two nights—a trio of Raymond Chandler's novels in one omnibus and a book about the Battle of Thermopylae. I slid off my sport coat and took off the shoulder holster with the Colt .32 in it. It had been my father's once and now it was mine. The pistol was flat, with art deco lines and sensibilities—like the Ghia, I fell in love with it at first sight. It didn't hurt that it seemed to be in every Bogie movie. I picked up my jacket, put it back on, and was off to Logan.

Chapter 2

Iparked in the long-term lot, made it into the terminal, and made my way through all the counters and the security checkpoint in short order. I stopped to present my ticket; then I was down the Jetway and into the plane itself. The door closed behind me, and I leaned back in my seat. I am not fond of flying. There is always some screaming baby or kindergartner kicking my seat. I don't like being trapped in my seat in some aluminum cylinder for hours on end. At least in the army they would open the doors and let us jump out.

The stewardess was wearing a blue skirt that showed enough leg to make me look up from Philip Marlowe's misadventures whenever she swished by. She brought food and drinks, and smiled at me with a smile that was all plastic and no real warmth. The movie was something about the guy from that disco movie, but now he was a sound effects man. It had conspiracies and guns and Philadelphia. It seemed frantic, and I preferred peeking into Marlowe's world. The dialogue was crisper and classier. At times, I tried to sleep, and mostly my ears hurt from the pressure.

The plane landed with a thump, and after a lot of waiting, I was emancipated into a terminal that had carpets of burnt umber. I walked up the Jetway, and this time no one in the terminal looked at me like I was a criminal. Now my hair was longer, and I had a beard. No one could see the scars, and I could pretend that they weren't there. I was wearing penny loafers with blue faded blue jeans, a white shirt, and a corduroy blazer that was technically fawn colored. My watch was a simple Timex, and the only jewelry I wore was my old dog tags and my old St. Michael medal. I wasn't religious, but he was the patron saint of paratroopers, and the combination of that medal and the dog tags got me through Vietnam. I followed the signs, and by the time I made my way to the street, there was a man in a dark suit and aviator glasses holding a sign with my name on it. I walked up to him and said, "I'm Roark." He nodded his mirrored head and his ample blond, layered hair.

He opened the door to a dark blue Lincoln that was big enough to land helicopters on. We took the expressway and then angled down into the city. It was early evening and dark had set. The closer we got to the city, the more it seemed the show was on. Hippies, punks, addicts, and cops; they were all out doing their part of the elaborate social dance on the street. The car pulled up to a hotel that was old and dripped class. The glass partition between us hissed down, and he told me what room to go to. He didn't get out and open the door for me. I wasn't a guest—I was the help.

I stepped outside. We were only a few nights from Halloween. In Boston, it was an Indian summer and warm. In San Francisco, I shivered on the sidewalk, wishing I had the trench coat that Leslie had given me for my last birthday.

I went into the hotel, slowing only to gauge where the elevators were. I made my way up to the room. I knocked. She opened the door to the suite.

"Mr. Roark. Our Boston attorney recommended you

quite highly." She was blonde, more Lauren Bacall than Farrah Fawcett. She was probably thirty and looked twenty-five. She took my hand in a firm grip that let me know how the tennis racquet must feel.

"I hope you mean Danny Sullivan?" I was conscious of my accent, Boston steam-rolled with U.S. Army Southern into something flat and vaguely East Coast. She sat in a wing chair in front of an unlit fireplace and gestured for me to sit across from her in a matching one. She held a file folder, and there were more next to her on a small table. There was a glass of white wine on the table, and her hair was perfect. She was wearing one of those pantsuits that only look good if they are expensive, and your body is long and lean. Hers was very expensive and looked very good. She crossed one long leg over the other, and I knew without being told that horses and tennis had been a major part of her upbringing.

"Dan Sullivan is a bright man." She was younger than Danny or me, but she owned everything that lay before her. The worst part was that she knew it. She made me feel like I was in the principal's office for writing dirty words on the boys' bathroom wall.

"He has a very bright future with us." I'd bet good money that she had graduated from Radcliffe or Vassar. Her voice had a huskiness that would have been cheap on anyone else.

"Us? Who are you?" She had a quality that would make a man become ruthless just to keep her happy. I was with her for two minutes, and I was sure of it.

"My name is Deborah Swift. My husband is Geoffrey Swift of the San Francisco Swifts, as in Swift Aeronautical."

"Oh, those Swifts, of course." Swift Aeronautical had been Swift Marine, which had made wooden PT boats for the navy in World War II. In Korea, they had graduated to bigger boats and parts for jet planes. By Vietnam, they had given up on the boats and just focused on parts for jets. Those parts had made the Swift family millions to keep their existing millions from getting lonely.

"My husband, despite his unlikely name, has a prospect of becoming the first Republican senator from the Bay Area in a long time."

"Bully for him." Her eyes were big and green and distracting.

"I would like to see that he succeeds. To that end, I require the services of someone who is capable and, more importantly, discreet. Dan Sullivan says that you are that person. Are you?" The big green eyes were focused on me, and I was aware that the two top buttons of her blouse were not buttoned and that pale flesh was showing in contrast to tanned skin.

"I am discreet, and I am capable. The caveat is that I am also somewhat moral, and there are things that I won't do."

She laughed.

"Good, I like a man with a sense of morals. However, Dan also told me that you frequently bend the rules." Her ears were perfectly shaped with diamond-accented lobes that you wanted to take between your lips, your teeth.

"I believe in right and wrong, and that doesn't always conform with the rules and regulations." She had a freckle at the beginning of the valley that was formed by the two buttons being undone on her blouse. She looked at the folder in her hands and looked up at me.

"Andrew 'Red' Roark, 10/13/1949, of Boston, Mass., attended Catholic high school in South Boston, a year and a half at the University of Rhode Island . . . Rhode Island?" She looked at me over the top of the folder. I shrugged. What could I say, I wanted to be an engineer, and it was close to the beach. "Voluntarily enlisted into the U.S. Army, February 1968 . . . voluntarily?" It was said the same way as "Rhode Island" was said, the way one might correct a particularly slow third grader. "Attended basic infantry and airborne training Fort Benning, Georgia, Army Special Forces training Fort Bragg, North Carolina, Military Assistance Command, Vietnam. Command and Control North, Republic of Vietnam." Cool green eyes looking down rifle sights at my face. "What was Command and Control North, Republic of Vietnam?" A breath and the freckles heaved, and I was slightly weak in the knees.

"I can't actually talk about all of that." She gave me a look that made me feel like I should be waiting in line for the swings at recess. There would not have been much point in talking about it. It was like all wars, only those who fought in it understood any of it. She made mention of the rank I had earned and the medals I had been awarded, but none of that meant much. Friends who were gone, scars that covered wounds that ached when it got cold, and dreams that came by to visit more than poor relatives looking for a handout. That is all the war meant now. Not much of a war to talk about in a hotel suite in San Francisco.

"Ooooh, it's secret. Honorable discharge 1972, Boston University for a semester, a few months off, and then the Boston Police Department for five years, all the time going to night school, almost eking out a degree. 1979, resigned from Boston Police Department, minutes before being fired for insubordination, and then off on your own as a private detective." Her green eyes zeroing in on my blue ones and me not having anywhere to look or to hide. "Is that accurate?"

"More or less." I didn't like having my life summed up like that. It sounded cheap.

"My father was a marine." After a pause, "He fought in

Korea." She said it in the same way that she summed up my life. Short and inexpensive.

"He came home from the war when I was a little girl." I nodded, not knowing what else to do or say. "He was home for a while and everything was wonderful, my parents dancing in the kitchen and songs on the radio all the time. It did not last long. One night he went out for a pack of cigarettes, and we never saw him again. My mother eventually remarried, and I took my stepfather's name. The best thing that my mother had to say about my father was that he was tall, and after a short time I stopped asking." Light flashed off of the diamonds in her earlobes, and she shifted her slim body in the wing chair, then one long leg over the other. "My husband is going to announce his candidacy soon. We hope that in time he can run for president." I had to stop for a second, because I was pretty sure that Reagan had it locked up until '84.

"We have an excellent chance of representing the state, but I am, of course, careful. I don't know what became of my father, but I would like you to find out. I do not want to read about any unpleasant surprises in the *Chronicle*." I nodded as though I had all the answers. If she was talking about the 1968 Democratic Convention, I could see where having a missing marine father might be a black spot to avoid. Now being a veteran was no longer considered a sin. "I hired a large firm out here, but they were not able to find much. They did trace my father to a town on Cape Cod, but the trail ran cold for them. That is why I needed you. You are local, and people will tell you things they won't tell a Pinkerton man from San Francisco."

"What do you hope I will find?"

"I want to know if there is anything to find. I want to know that my father hasn't done anything that can hurt Geoffrey."

"Your father, the former marine?"

"Yes." Breathless, now more Ingrid Bergman than Bacall, more vulnerability than sex appeal. "I would hate to
think that he committed a crime or is some gin-soaked veteran slowly dying on a barstool somewhere."

"Why do you need me? Pinkerton is more than capable.
If they didn't find anything, there probably isn't anything
to find."

"You are one of them. You probably root for the Red
Sox and think that Manhattan clam chowder is basically
clam minestrone. That is why I need you. You understand
the lay of the land, but more than that you speak the same
way the locals do. I doubt that the Pinkerton men did."

"You think that people on the Cape might not open up
to strangers from California?"

"That is part of it. I also think that they didn't understand the terrain that they were operating on."

"Okay, that makes sense. How did you establish that he
has something to do with Cape Cod?"

"The Pinkerton men started with records from the Vet-
erans Administration. They found an address in Hyannis,
Massachusetts, where the VA sent a few checks." She was
the type of woman who couldn't bring herself to just say
Hyannis.

"When was that?"

"In 1968. Prior to that it was Las Vegas, before that Los
Angeles, even Seattle for a brief time. Three checks in 1968
were sent to an address in Hyannis, Massachusetts, and
then nothing. He stopped getting checks from the VA."

"Why do you think that there will be something poten-
tially damaging in his past?"

She sighed and then laughed. "You do not know much
about politics, do you, Mr. Roark? Everything is a potential scandal; even simple or innocent things can turn out to
be damaging."

"Like a missing father."

"Exactly. Are you going to take the case?"

"Sure. I'm between jobs." She smiled, and it reminded me of Danny's smile. She handed me a large manila envelope with the Pinkerton name on it in one corner. I took it, and it weighed as much as a first edition of *Gone with the Wind*.

"That is everything that Pinkerton came up with. They used a great deal of paper to say very little." She handed me another smaller envelope.

"That is five thousand dollars. That includes your retainer, fee for coming out here, a week's worth of salary, and some for expenses. If you need anything else, or if you have expenses, contact Mr. Sullivan. He has been temporarily retained to represent our interests on the East Coast. He will also see that you are paid on a weekly basis should things drag on. There is a ticket waiting for you at the Pan Am counter. My man should have you there in time to catch the red-eye." She stood and stuck out a cool hand. I stood and shook hers, then turned and walked away.

Chapter 3

The elevator and the lobby were the same. The driver and the car were also the same. He drove me out to the airport without a word. I had hoped to see the wharf and go to a bar, the Golden Gate Park or something, but instead it was tour through the Richmond and then a bit of expressway. The envelope with the money sat substantially in my breast pocket, and the file was in the postman's bag. I wanted to look at it, but somehow it didn't seem right inside the car.

He pulled up in the departure lane, and I stepped out onto the pavement and made my way into the glass and concrete monstrosity that the city of San Francisco considered its airport. Inside, I made my way to the airline check-in and then to the gate. Along the way, I found a bar that was able to give me a double Dewar's on the rocks. I read some of the history of the Battle of Thermopylae, looking up to see the occasional pretty lady walk by. Few places are more depressing than airport bars.

I wanted to look at the folder from Pinkerton, but airport bars aren't the sort of place where you should do that sort of thing. There is never any privacy and never any space. I took out a Lucky and lit it instead. The first sip of scotch and a cigarette work well together.

Most of my cases are either divorce or insurance fraud. There is some missing persons work, but it is usually the husband who went to the corner store for a gallon of milk five years ago and didn't come back. Sometimes it is the wife who goes to the store; sometimes it is a teenager who has run away. In most cases, people hire me to find someone because they care about them and need to know what happened. Sometimes it is about child support, but usually there is some feeling there. I had never been hired before to find someone because a budding politician didn't want a scandal.

The metallic voice called my flight number after the Battle for Thermopylae had ended, and I was on my second scotch. I lifted the heavy canvas bag and made my way to my gate. The stewardess welcomed me onto the plane with the same robotic greeting that is the trademark of their industry. I found my seat and strapped in. People filed in, stopping to stow their bags and ease into a seat. The door shut at last, and we hurtled down the runway and lurched into the sky.

I waited until the stewardess brought me a scotch; then I opened the large folder that I had taken out of my bag. On top was a black and white snapshot of a thin young man in Marine Corps dress blues. It was the official yearbook photo taken right after graduating from Parris Island. The soft glow from the small overhead light didn't reveal anything other than he was young, with high cheekbones and a slightly dimpled chin. There was also a photo of the same young man with longer dark hair, in utilities with two other marines, all posing with their rifles. Last was a picture of the same young man with a crew cut, wearing khaki pants and a madras shirt, holding a little blond girl.

His name, according to the file, was Charles Edgar Hammond. He was born in June 1932, not far from San Diego, California. He married Mary Ellen Frazier right after graduation. He joined the Marine Corps in August of 1950 and found himself in Korea shortly after that. Mary Ellen gave birth to Deborah in March 1951. Hammond wound up at the Chosin Reservoir—he was wounded but managed to survive. He was promoted to sergeant by the time both sides sat down to talk and agree to keep the war but not fight anymore. He was rotated stateside and was posted in San Diego at the navy base in Coronado. Shortly after he was discharged, he and Mary Ellen were visiting her parents with Deborah. Charles Hammond told his wife that he had to go to the store for cigarettes and never came back. It didn't take Mary Ellen long to get a divorce and find a job as a legal secretary to a patent attorney. She married the patent attorney eighteen months later. He was two decades older than Mary Ellen, but he wasn't the type to go out for cigarettes, and he could afford the best schools for Deborah, whom he adopted.

After that, the file turned into random pieces of paper that told the rest of the story. Some were from the VA, check stubs or notices. Some were expense reports from the Pinkerton detectives. They had followed the VA checks to Los Angeles, where they found the transient hotel that Charlie Hammond had lived in for several months. They couldn't find anyone who had even been there in 1954, much less anyone who knew him.

From 1955 to 1958, the VA checks went to a series of cheap apartment houses in Los Angeles. According to the Social Security office, Charlie had a lot of low-wage jobs that lasted for a few months at a time and never for more than six months. In 1959, Charlie moved to Las Vegas,

Nevada, where he apparently worked in a casino that no longer existed, and none of the employees they tracked down knew him. Charlie was in Las Vegas until 1965. Las Vegas was also the last time that Charlie paid into Social Security, paid taxes, or seemed to have a job. Early in 1966, Charlie was getting his mail in a transient hotel in Seattle, Washington. He dropped off of the radar screen and reemerged in the fall of 1966 back in Los Angeles. In 1968, three checks were sent to a P.O. box in Hyannis, Mass. There was no VA paperwork to explain why Hyannis or why for just three months. By the end of 1968, he was in San Francisco, his mail going to a P.O. box in Haight-Ashbury. By 1972, Charlie's VA checks started getting returned to the VA. Charlie didn't go to his mother's funeral in 1973. Charlie never responded to the divorce proceedings, and the detective the patent attorney hired in 1956 couldn't find him. All I had was a P.O. box on the Cape. It was, as we say professionally, pretty thin.

It had taken me two scotches to go through the file. Pinkerton had earned their money. They had sent detectives to any place that Charlie Hammond might have ever lived, visited, or seemingly even passed through. The P.O. boxes didn't help. P.O. boxes were easy if the person you are looking for is using one currently. You sit on the box and wait. They show up to get the mail, and you have found your missing person. It is like magic. But almost twenty years later, P.O. boxes and transient hotels are dead ends. Charlie's trail was as cold as last Christmas.

I turned off the overhead light and tried to sleep. The seat was uncomfortable, and I woke up every fifteen minutes or so. When I finally gave up and admitted that it wasn't going to happen, I had a sharp pain in my neck, and my mouth felt like someone had covered it with carpet from an hourly motel.

The captain made his announcement, and the seat belt

light went on. The stewardess came by to make sure that we were sitting up and that we were not recklessly leaving our trays down. The plane banked and I could see Boston Harbor, the gas tanks, and Quincy. Then I could only see water and buildings; then we touched down with a hard thump. As the plane taxied up to the gate, I was putting everything away in my canvas sack. I stood up when we stopped, as much to stretch my stiff, abused back as to retrieve my corduroy blazer. I made my way up the Jetway and through the terminal. My head hurt and I needed a shower.

I blinked at the bright October sun and shivered slightly in the cool morning air. I found a Lucky from a pack in my jacket that wasn't too crushed, and lit it. I felt good to be back in Boston. It always feels good to be back in Boston.

I made my way through the maze of cars until I found the Ghia. It started and I made my way to the parking lot attendant's booth. He took my money, leaving me to fight the traffic, as everyone on the East Coast was trying to get into the city to go to work. I started listening to the news, but that was just depressing. It took me almost an hour to get home, and I managed to get the Ghia into the parking spot behind my building. Pumpkins were on sale and jack-o'-lanterns were starting to appear on steps. I locked the car and made my way upstairs to the apartment.

I opened the door and let myself in. I only recently stopped half expecting her to be in the apartment. It was still half an apartment. I dropped the bag on a chair in the small living room. I thought about making coffee but opted for a shower and toothbrush instead. After the shower, it was bed and a few hours of sleep.

Chapter 4

When I woke up, it was late afternoon. I went over and paid attention to the blinking lights on the machine. None was important enough to make me pick up the phone. I put the coffee on and took the Pinkerton file out of the canvas bag. I took the file into the kitchen, where I poured coffee. I padded back out to the living room and put The Rolling Stones on the turntable. Mick Jagger offered to introduce himself to me, mentioning that he was a man of wealth and taste. At least one of us was.

I sat at the kitchen table and drank coffee, reading back through the files. This time, unlike on the plane, I made notes on a yellow legal pad with a blue felt pen. It took a pot of coffee, two pieces of toast, a half a pack of Luckies, and a couple hours to go through it all again. The salient points were that Charlie Hammond had been in the Korean War. He had acquitted himself well and come home with some medals: a Silver Star, a Bronze Star, and couple of Purple Hearts that looked good against the dress blue uniform. He had walked out on his wife and young daughter. He kicked around the West Coast; then all traces of him stopped in 1972. Ten years ago. That was it on Charlie Hammond. Pinkerton had talked to everyone and anyone who they could. No one knew anything about Charlie Hammond.

I got up and went to the phone in the living room. I called Danny's office, and his secretary was able to find him after a short wait. Danny suggested a bar not far from his office near the John Hancock Tower. I showered and put on jeans, cordovan loafers, a white shirt, the Colt .32 in its shoulder rig, and a corduroy sport coat that was the darker cousin of the one I wore to San Francisco. The weather looked nice but cooler, and I grabbed the fawn-colored trench coat Leslie had given me. I didn't feel like driving. Parking was more trouble than walking over to the bar.

The sunshine outside was brittle, the way it seems to be in New England in the fall. I would like to believe that I could smell smoke from a fire in the air, but it was only the diesel fumes from a passing bus. It wasn't chilly yet, but in a week or two, fall would become an unpleasant prelude to winter. I like fall and, until mid-January, I like winter, but by then I am sick of the cold, the snow, and slush.

I walked down Commonwealth Avenue heading toward the Common but turned down a parallel street heading toward Newbury Street. I made my way through the streets, stopping to wait for the lights to be in my favor. Anything else would have been madness. The bar was more or less where Danny said it would be. It was also three steps down from the street and had black and white pictures of old Boston Celtics and Red Sox. It had a bay window, tables, chairs, booths, and a vaguely nautical feel to it. It was quarter to five, and the place was two-thirds full with the people who slip out of work early for a drink. The bar was already loud and filling with smoke. I made my way through the swell of put-together men and women to the bar, where Danny was sitting. There was a glass of scotch with four ice cubes and two fingers in it in front of him.

I slid into the seat next to him, beating out a man in a blue suit who I would have sworn had a perm. Golden Curls shot me a dirty look, hunched his shoulders, and moved down the bar toward the corner. He might have muttered "asshole" under his breath, and I might have cared in some other lifetime.

"Andy, how's the boy?" Danny punched me lightly on the shoulder.

"Danny, did you get good news, or have you been in this place since lunch?" Danny was the type of guy who drinks, drinks a lot, but doesn't get drunk. It has something to do with that computer he calls a brain.

"Our friend in San Francisco called. She is pleased with you, which means that she is pleased with me." He drank some of his scotch and waited while I ordered from the bartender, who also looked like he had a perm. His curls weren't golden, though, they were brown. Was I missing out on a male fashion trend?

"She is pleased that I took the job?" I wanted to say case. Philip Marlowe would have called it a case. On the other hand, Marlowe had a lot more class than I did. The bartender brought my Löwenbräu and pilsner glass, which I ignored. When he went away, Danny started to talk again. He was the type who never talked business in front of waiters or bartenders.

"She called me this afternoon. She said that you were the right man for the job. She then said that I was to draw one thousand dollars a week from an account at Old Stone Bank for expenses and your pay for as long as you are gainfully employed on her case. You will report your progress to me and send the report to me, which I will forward to her." I nodded my understanding of his instructions.

"You must be digging up a lot of dirt or burying something big." There was a question somewhere in there, and I found myself wondering if Danny was actually off the clock. Knowing Danny, he would find a way to turn all twenty-four hours of the day into billable hours. I was also noticing a very pretty brunette in the mirror behind the bar.

"No, it's nothing like that. It's a missing person case."

"Who's missing? Not the husband?" He sounded alarmed. The brunette was lighting a cigarette and looking bored while Golden Curls talked at her.

"Her father is missing." Danny had finished his scotch and was motioning for the bartender to bring us two more. I lit a cigarette and contemplated the brunette in her light gray jacket and cream-colored blouse. The beer arrived in front of me, and Brown Curls took away the unused pilsner glass.

"Her father, the patent attorney? I thought he was dead." He finished what was left in his old glass of scotch and slid it toward the bartender's side of the bar.

"Nope, that was her stepfather, and yes, he is dead. Her real father was a marine in Korea. He came home from the war to wife and daughter, went out for a pack of smokes, and you guessed it . . . never came back." The Löwenbräu was cold, and the brunette was laughing at something Golden Curls said. I did not take it as a good sign for me.

"She isn't your type." Danny was looking in the mirror, too. He also knew me pretty well.

"Whaddaya mean, not my type?" I wasn't even sure I had a type.

"She's not some intellectual liberal grad student or some sensitive arts type." He was smiling a little, not much of a smile.

"How do you know?"

"She is a contract attorney in my firm, and she would eat a sap like you for an appetizer." He was good at building a case.

"I meant, how do you know what my type is?"

"Leslie. Remember all those dinners at the house? Remember how Maryanne thought you two were going to get married? Remember how she told you not to screw it up?" Danny was allegedly brutal in cross-examination. I had enough cop friends who almost didn't want to talk to me when they found out that Danny and I were friends.

"Can we change the subject?" I didn't like being reminded of the fact that Leslie walked out because I am hard to live with and apparently easy to live without.

When we first met we would talk about all of the things you talk about when the relationship is new. Childhood, family, early happy memories. We decided to get a place together and were lucky to find our apartment. It wasn't big and the building, an old brownstone, was in perpetual disrepair, but the rent was reasonable and we had a view of the river between buildings. There was a lot of joy in picking our furniture, building bookshelves, buying books. At first it was great to stay in and make dinner together. There was a lot of laughter and a lot of trying to see who could get out of their clothes first.

We made love at night. Then I would dream about Vietnam and wake up muttering. Kicking at sheets and blankets, sweating after fighting the imaginary demons of my bygone war. The war that society didn't want to talk about and the army said that I could not talk about. I didn't want to talk to Leslie about it. I didn't want to talk to her about the men whom I had killed and even worse, the friends who had been killed. I didn't want her to think of me that way. Soon, the silences grew longer and more frequent. Soon I didn't want to talk about work; I didn't want to talk about much. Talking led to arguing about my not talking. In the end she chose absence over silence and left me.

"Okay, so tell me about the case." Danny seemed interested, and the brunette lady shark lawyer looked like she

was interested in Golden Curls's stories. I brought Danny
up to speed on the thinnest case ever.

"I am looking for a Korean War veteran, a marine, the
last trace of whom was in 1972." I tried to wash the state-
ment down with cold Löwenbräu, but it stuck in my
throat like dust.

"1972, that was ten years ago. You were in Vietnam."
He said it as though my being in Vietnam had any bearing
on anything. A woman with honey-colored hair who was
sitting next to Danny cocked an ear at the Vietnam thing.
I smiled like it was a joke. "So, what happened in 1972?"

"That is the last time that he collected his check from
the VA."

"Here in Boston?" Danny was motioning to the bartender, and I was beginning to wonder if it was going to be
one of those nights that leads to one of those days where I
wake up wondering why I don't learn.

"No, he got his last check in San Francisco." The
woman with honey-colored hair was trying to listen without seeming to listen.

"So, why did she hire you? Wouldn't someone out there
be better suited?" Danny slid a bottle toward me, and I
slid an empty back toward him.

"She did. She hired Pinkerton." The woman with honey-
colored hair was wearing a dark jacket over a cream-colored
blouse, probably another killer lawyer who Danny knew.

"Pinkerton. Are they still detectives? I thought all they
did now was security work." He was smiling his three-
scotch crooked smile.

"Nope, they still do detective work. I have a *Gone with
the Wind*–size file to prove it." The woman with honey-
colored hair and the cream blouse under her blue jacket
was leaning closer.

"What does she think you can do that they can't? They
are a pretty big outfit with a lot of resources."

"Her father got a few checks out on the Cape in the late sixties. Pinkerton looked into it, but she felt from their report that people on the Cape wouldn't talk to them because they weren't local." I took another pull on my beer.

"Where will you start?" He was all ears now.

"I'll go to the post office where he got his checks and see if they can tell me who owned the box in 1968. Then I will see if they are still around." The woman with honey-colored hair in the cream blouse with a dark jacket also had on a string of pearls, and I wanted to send her a drink.

"That is an awfully long shot." Danny, master of the obvious, had struck again.

"I know, but it is all that is left. That and going to the VA and spending a lot of money to see if anyone knows anything."

"Don't you think that Pinkerton tried all that?"

"I am sure they did, but their reports indicate that people really didn't say much to them at all. They might just talk to me."

"Well, when you are not being an asshole, you do have a winning way about you."

"Thanks, I wish I could say the same of you."

Danny swirled some scotch around in his glass and then took a drink of it. Ice cubes clinked against the glass, and he put it back down on the bar.

"Do you think there is a chance that he is out on the Cape somewhere?"

"I don't know for sure, but I can tell you that he isn't in San Francisco or Las Vegas, probably not even on the West Coast. Pinkerton would have picked up on that."

"How do you know he isn't dead?" Danny was not too subtly slipping into cross-examination mode. The woman with the honey-colored hair was barely even trying to look as though she wasn't listening.

"He might be, but I doubt it. He was in the service and

he was fingerprinted. If his body turned up, they would have printed him, and the VA would have sprung for the burial. There would have been some sort of record of that. Pinkerton would have picked up on that." In the bar mirror, she looked to have brown eyes, but in the low light they could have been hazel.

"Or his body never turned up?"

"That's true. Whatever he was up to, it probably wasn't legal, and people doing illegal things tend to get dead sooner than straight people."

"They also tend to end up in shallow, unmarked graves more often as well."

"Like Jimmy Hoffa," I said.

"Like Jimmy Hoffa," he agreed.

"I don't think that this guy was in Hoffa's league." The woman with honey-colored hair was drinking white wine.

"What do you think he was into?" Danny had also noticed the woman with honey-colored hair and shot her a smile in the mirror.

"I don't know. Could have been anything. He could have been mobbed up or in the rackets. He was in Vegas, so I am sure that gambling wouldn't be a stretch. Drugs are always a possibility, too." She smiled back at Danny, but it was a smile that acknowledged her transgressions at the bar.

"If he was in Vegas in the sixties and seventies, he couldn't have pulled on a one-armed bandit without tripping on someone who was mobbed up." Danny would know, given who many of his clients were. Danny's clients were the type of mobsters who could buy anything, anyone—cops, judges, politicians—and when they couldn't go to jail, they paid Danny.

Danny could park his Cadillac in neighborhoods that cops couldn't go into alone. There were bars in Southie that I wouldn't go into without a shotgun, where Danny never had to pay for his whiskey. Danny was a good lawyer who kept a lot of people out of jail and who had a lot of very powerful friends. The Mercedes in the garage and private schools for the girls came at a high price.

"Or it could be he is another vet who came home from a shitty war and drank himself to death while no one was looking." I had known enough guys who had done it.

"Like you?" Danny wasn't smiling anymore. Danny had told me often enough what a fuckup I was. He had hated it when I joined the cops but lost it when I quit. He had yelled at me, saying if I had stuck with it I could have risen through the ranks. He frequently reminded me that I was smart, that I could have been anything. I would have made a great lawyer. In the end, I think he felt guilty that I went to Vietnam and he didn't. Sometimes when he got drunk enough he would talk about feeling bad being anti-war while I was over there. He thought if I just grew up, married the right girl, and had a family it would all be fine.

"I didn't try and drink myself to death. I cut loose a little, but I adjusted all right." I had a few rough nights, but that was understandable.

"That isn't what I am talking about. You went on a couple tears, but more than that, you were just quiet. You wouldn't say anything sometimes for hours at a time. You used to disappear. We'd be in a bar or at a party, and one second you would be there and the next I wouldn't see you for a couple of days." He was all business now. It was true. I remember one night, we were at a party in Quincy, and I had to get out of the place. I went and told Danny and Maryanne that I was going to the bathroom and walked out the kitchen door into the night air.

I walked up into the Quincy Quarry and started moving

down the trails. I rubbed dirt into my face and hands to camouflage them. I moved quietly, slowly, the way I had been taught, off of the trail. I moved around kids making out and around kids smoking weed. I slid around all of them like water around rocks. For a short time, I was back doing what they had trained me to do, the only thing I had ever really been good at doing. I once was so close to an NVA that I could hear his cigarette crackle softly when he inhaled. He never knew I was there.

When I woke the next morning, cold and damp in some scrub, there was a thick fog. For a few seconds, I thought that I was in Vietnam by the Ho Chi Minh Trail. I would wake up in the mist. You couldn't see anything, and that was the scariest part. You didn't know if the men hunting you were just a few feet away. You didn't know if they had gotten close or not. I had hated the mornings.

That morning in Quincy, I woke up cold and scared. It was like one of the bad dreams from the war. Instead of being in school naked, I was in the jungle. I didn't have my Swedish K gun with the big silencer. I didn't have my 9mm Browning or my knife. No grenades or Claymore mines. No radio, no nothing. I was just cold and wet, and the enemy was out there. But he wasn't. I was in a quarry outside of Boston covered in dirt, with twigs in my beard and hair. I was scared of phantoms, of my past sins. I had readjusted just fine.

In the end, I had to learn to live with it. I dropped out of school. Political Theory is a lot less interesting if you have debated it with guns and grenades. I saw an ad in the *Globe*—the police department was hiring. I almost had a degree, a good war record, and a couple of medals that didn't mean anything to anyone but the hiring board. The academy was drudgery, but it passed. My training officer had been in Korea—he didn't say much to me. He smoked a lot, drank more, and didn't take shit from anyone on the street. I saw more than one guy get his head bounced off a wall or the hood of a cruiser.

I loved the street. It was electric. You never knew from one call to the next what you were going to get. Some nights it was just one brawl after another. Some nights I got the shit knocked out of me. I was cut with a box knife and had a bottle broken over my head, but in the end, I could sleep most nights. Once I put on the uniform, I lost the feeling of waiting for things, bad things, to happen to me. I had regained a measure of control. By the time I realized that it was bullshit, I was on my way out. I told off a few too many people who had more drag than me, and a fistfight with a sergeant ended a career without much future. Like I said, I adjusted just fine.

Danny finished his scotch and mumbled something about Maryanne and the kids. He threw some money down on the bar and told me to call him when I had learned anything. I said sure, and with that he was gone. I still had half a Löwenbräu and was in no rush. I lit a cigarette and looked in the mirror, but the woman with honey-colored hair was gone. I wasn't her type, anyway.

Chapter 5

I woke up the next morning and got myself cleaned up. I had coffee and toast, and looked through the *Globe*. Nothing in it looked good. The *Globe* had news about the president increasing the marines' mission in Lebanon. I was dressed in jeans, a blue oxford shirt, the Colt .32, and a corduroy jacket, all of which went under Leslie's trench coat. I got in the Ghia and headed toward Route 3 South to the Cape. The drive down 3 South starts off in the high, granite walls of an area that two hundred years ago provided slabs of granite for the cities of the Northeast, leads past Route 24, and eventually flattens out to the beginning of the sandy arm that is Cape Cod.

When I passed Route 24, it was obvious that fall was in full effect and until the ride flattened out into pine trees, the foliage was red and yellow. It was the type of fall day where the sun was playing tag with the clouds. Warm enough when the sun was out, but if it stayed behind the clouds for too long, I had to coax heat out of the Ghia's heater. It was anybody's guess, but the weatherman had said that the sun would give way to all-too-familiar New England wind and rain. It was the type of weather that I loved and one of the reasons I couldn't live anywhere else. That and the Red Sox.

The classical radio station was playing Dvorak, and it was nice to be driving somewhere other than the mad traffic of the city. Occasionally the program host would come on with his deep voice, sounding like he had smoked a pound of weed before the program. Nice and mellow. Letting you know that no matter what shit was going down, he had the classical music locked down for you.

In Vietnam, our radio guy Donnie Hicks had been like that. It didn't matter what shit we were into, Donnie's deep basso would rumble down the handset to you when he was a Covey Rider, a sort of Forward Air Controller just for SOG. "Be cool, baby. We got some fast movers coming in. Gonna burn up some shit, so you best be getting to the LZ an' get with the slicks. You dig?" Hearing Donnie's voice on the other end of the radio was like taking a golf ball–sized Valium. Whatever was going down, you just got calmer. Mellower. You knew shit was just gonna work out, because he told you so.

Donnie was a legendary radio man on teams. When I first got to Nam, I was lucky enough to work with him. He was a radio artist. AK-47 rounds would be snapping all around, and Donnie would be just chatting with the Covey Rider, circling above us in his little prop plane. You'd hear Donnie, "Um, baby, we in some shit down here. What you got on deck for me? Shit yeah, F-4s be nice." Like he was discussing blondes or brunettes instead of jets with napalm and rockets. "Uh-huh . . . Cobras . . . yeah, send them, too. Ain't you got no Sky Raiders for me, baby?" Shit, yeah. Donnie was the living embodiment of Zen cool, and his calm saved my ass more than once. I heard that Donnie stayed in the army. He said that Vietnam was safer than the South Side of Chicago.

I drove along, enjoying the scenery and listening to

Dvorak. The road hissed along under the car, and life was okay. My head hurt a little from the night before with Danny, but not too badly. I had taken an Anacin when I got up and hadn't needed an Alka-Seltzer, which was reserved for New Year's Day types of hangover. The hissing of the tires coupled with the engine and the radio made for a soothing noise.

I drove over the Bourne Bridge, marveling as always at the WPA-era construction and details, over the Cape Cod Canal, and entered into the rotary. Exiting the rotary, I followed the canal until it was time to turn onto Route 6 and, after a few twists and turns, into Hyannis. I turned onto Main Street and followed it up in one direction and then turned down it in the other. I was near The Steamship Authority, where Leslie and I had taken the ferry out to Nantucket on our last vacation. We had been early enough for the ferry that we had been able to get breakfast at a diner on Main Street. It had been nice sitting at the counter on yellow vinyl-topped stools. They were the type that as a kid I would spin myself around on until my head hurt with dizziness.

It had been a good vacation, almost the calm before the storm. If I had paid attention, I might have seen the signs. The desire to make happy memories, ones that would last, so that she had good times to remember. The sun had been nice and the beaches beautiful. We had made love in the afternoons just back from the beach, smelling of Coppertone. Her skin tasted like salt from the ocean. The nights were cool and I slept without nightmares. It was like I was normal for a week.

The diner was still there, and my stomach was rumbling in a way that let me know it expected food after a night of drinking. I found a spot up from the diner and parked. I slid a couple of quarters into the meter and headed toward breakfast and more coffee. The storefronts were decorated with orange and black streamers. Everywhere there were cardboard ghosts and goblins.

I could smell fried eggs, mixing with the fall air that was coming off of the water. The leaves on the trees planted along Main Street were shades of red, yellow, and orange. I was heading away from the post office, but I was hungry and stalling. I wanted eggs, bacon, and bad coffee, with toast that was only buttered in the center of each piece. I wanted time to think about what I was going to say to whatever faceless postal employee was at the counter.

I went into the diner. Most of the breakfast crowd had left, and lunch wasn't for a long couple of hours. There was a middle-aged waitress straight out of central casting, smoking a cigarette and leaning against one side of the counter. In a booth, two old women were talking about someone named Justine who had run off with someone named Rico. I was jealous I didn't know anyone named Rico. Behind the waitress, I could see the grill and the guy working it.

I sat down at the counter and waited for the waitress to peel herself off her end of it to take my order. She put a vinyl-covered menu down in front of me as though she were swatting a fly with it.

"Coffee?" She half barked the question at me.

"Please." She went to the Bunn and poured me a cup from the half of a pot that had been sitting there since the end of the breakfast rush. She put it down and slid a little dish with sugar packets and some pink packets of sweetener toward me, along with a small tin pitcher of cream. I ignored the cream and the sugar.

"Know what you want?" I don't think it was me she disliked, just the world in general.

"Two eggs over easy, corned beef hash, and rye toast."

She didn't bother to write it down. She picked up the fly-swatting menu that I had ignored and pivoted on her heel away from me. The place had either lost its charm in the off-season, or it had just looked a whole lot better with Leslie in it. Leslie, whose smile was warm and bright, indicative of the person within. Leslie, who toward the end hadn't smiled much at me but had a lot of tears. Leslie, who had accused me of shutting her off. Shutting her out. Leslie, who got sick of the silences, the waking up in the middle of the night, because I was wrestling with the demons in my sleep.

In the beginning we had been in love. Everything love should be, warm, affectionate. We would talk about books, movies, cooking, my new passion. I remember that we laughed a lot and it felt good. Rainy days, sitting on the couch, drinking strong coffee, and reading the Sunday *Times* or *Globe,* I felt like maybe, just maybe I had a shot at being normal. Just like everyone else. Like the stain left on me by my part of the war would wash off because of her love. Looking back, it must have been an awful lot of pressure for her to bear. It wasn't enough that I was asking her to be my lover but also my salvation.

I wanted to believe that she got sick of the weird hours, or the fact that I carried a gun, or that I occasionally came home bruised. I think she would have put up with all of it if I had told her about any of it. If I had just let her in a little more. In the end, I wore her down with silence about the things that I couldn't or wouldn't talk to her about. In the end, those became the things that mattered.

It hadn't always been bad. The first year had been great. The best of my life maybe. We had met by chance in a used bookstore. I had left the cops and was a private detective, so I was looking for some detective fiction to show me how to do it. I spotted *The Raymond Chandler Omnibus* of

Philip Marlowe novels. *The Friends of Eddie Coyle* was coming home, too. There were a couple of Ross Macdonald novels in the pile.

In that same aisle was a girl in jeans and a sweatshirt standing on tiptoes, trying to reach the top shelf. Her hair was short by the standards of the day and when I offered to help her, she fixed me with dazzling blue eyes. She assessed me and I must have been judged acceptable because she favored me with a pearly smile. I handed her the book and she agreed to go for coffee. I couldn't believe that she had agreed to coffee and then a few days later a date.

She was a grad student at Northeastern, working on her PhD in English. She was focusing on Private Detective as the new, urban American cowboy. How as we moved into the cities after the Depression we stopped romanticizing cowboys, but we needed some violent paladin, not beholden to the rules. A man without family, without ties, without limitations, who could do what needed to be done. The private eye was the new cowboy. Wyatt Earp, Bat Masterson, and Doc Holliday had given way to Marlowe, Spenser, and Nick Charles.

In a lot of ways, it was as though she started dating her thesis. Except that I was no hero. I was a mess who went to sleep, ended up in Vietnam, and woke up sweating and fighting with the bedding. I didn't talk about it. I couldn't tell her about Vietnam. She was perfect, unmarred, and my sins were graphic, my hands would never be clean. In the end the gulf between us, the silence grew too wide. Then she left. There were no letters, no phone calls. She was gone and I ended up living in half of an apartment.

The food came and was what diner food should be: greasy, good, and life-sustaining. The coffee wasn't bad. I was expecting something that had been sitting in the urn for hours, but it was actually fresh. After I had finished, I realized the headache was gone and that I was ready to face the day. The waitress brought the check, and I put money down to cover it and the tip.

"Anything else, hon?" She picked up the bills and the check.

"Where's the post office from here?" I asked.

"Take a right and head up the street three blocks. You can't miss it; it has *U.S. Post Office* written on it." Her delivery was dry, and the sarcasm was not lost on me.

"Thanks, I need some stamps so I can mail you your tip." I left her a couple of singles anyway.

Chapter 6

The sun was mostly out by now, but it was anemic and stingy with its warmth. The gulls were circling overhead, riding thermals and making a racket as they whirled around. I couldn't look at them the same way anymore after having watched *The Birds*. There was enough of an off-shore breeze that I actually buttoned my trench coat. Normal people were out going about their normal business, making almost as much of a racket as the gulls. I wondered idly if any of them were armed or hung over or had been in a war? They all seemed so normal that I doubted it.

I passed a Chinese restaurant with a sign that told me it made the best Scorpion Bowls on the Cape. I passed a used bookstore. Across the street was an army-navy surplus store. I didn't need any more surplus from the army, so I kept moving. I passed about a hundred shops selling the crap that the tourists buy: T-shirts, plastic lobsters, pirate figurines.

The post office was a large, brick structure that screamed of WPA-era architecture and construction. It was large, imposing, and oddly out of place in a seaside town on the Cape. It looked more like one of the old public schools in Boston or a library, but here it dominated a block of Main Street.

Inside the lobby, the building had the opposite effect. It was cramped, lit by fluorescent lights; a bank of mailboxes crowded most of the lobby. The counter had four windows, but just like every bank, there were only two people working. The first was a pinched-face woman in her late forties. The other was a burly man in his late thirties, with starburst veins in his nose and the hint of a tattoo peeking down from his short-sleeve uniform shirt. I went to his window and ordered a book of stamps. When he reached into the register, I could make out a red bayonet held by a wing.

"173rd?" I tried to ask the question casually. He looked up, a little startled.

"Yeah, a lifetime ago. You?"

"No, I wasn't a Sky Soldier . . . were you there?" He looked at me for what seemed like a hard minute.

"Yeah. You?"

"Yeah, I was." I named a few of the bigger towns near where we had operated but refrained from telling him what I had done. I was finding that after the war there were a lot of guys saying they were Special Forces. Most of them were just saying it. I didn't want to be mistaken for one of them.

"Is there a good place to get lunch around here?"

"Yeah, Chinese place down the street."

"Maybe I'll see you there?" I put a fifty-dollar bill down on the counter, took my stamps, and walked out.

The restaurant was dimly lit with a faux Chinese motif and red vinyl booths. The place was littered with silk brocade, wooden dragons, screens, and a Buddha or two. The bar was left over from whatever it had been before but now was painted black. I was halfway through my second Löwenbräu when he walked in. He saw me and came over.

"You forgot your change." He slid some bills and coins across the bar to me.

"Let me buy you a beer?" He looked at me, trying to figure out what I was all about. "Let me buy you a beer and some lunch and tell you why I am here. If you don't like what you hear, you can walk out, and that will be the end of it. If you don't walk out, you will get a free lunch and might get to help a little girl find her long-lost father."

"I won't do nothing illegal." There was something angry and weary behind his eyes.

"I'm not asking you to. I'm just trying to track down a missing vet for his daughter. Nothing more than that."

"What are you, a private eye?" I nodded and slid one of my cards, the one with an oversized magnifying glass on it, to him. "How can I help?" He motioned to the bartender, who brought him a beer.

"My client's father came home from Korea and walked out on his family. I have hit nothing but dead ends. The only thing left is the fact that he got his VA checks sent to a P.O. box in your post office for a few months in 1968." He was sipping his beer and nodding as I went on. "I want to know who was renting that P.O. box at that time in 1968. I also need to know where they are now."

"I can find out who was renting it but can only tell you so much. They might have moved or died or whatever." He was looking intently at his beer.

"Anything would be helpful. Right now, this guy is pretty much a ghost. It is really important to his little girl that she finds him again." I couldn't tell if I was laying it on thick.

"Okay, give me the box number." I told him.

"I'll meet you up the street at a bar called the Salty Dog. It is a dive, but the beer is cold." He told me where to find the bar, and we agreed to meet there after his shift at 4:30.

Hyannis is a nice enough town, but it isn't so interesting that you can easily kill three and a half hours in it. I went into every bookstore they had, all two of them. Then the public library and even the gun store by the bus station. The only thing I ended up buying was a pack of cigarettes. I avoided all the places selling plastic lobsters and ship-in-a-bottle kits.

I walked down by the waterfront and looked at the mix of sailboats and cabin cruisers that weren't quite nice enough to be dry-docked or to head to the Caribbean for the winter. They were the hand-me-downs of the boating world. The teak was worn and the nice stain had faded. The brass was dull and had greenish spots. They were the type of boats that I would have had if I had the money for a boat.

The fishing boats were heading into port, followed by clouds of wheeling, turning gulls. Somehow, they were better, easier to look at. They were just as old and run-down, maybe more so, but they were being used. The men on those boats worked them; the boats still served a purpose. I took one last look and turned away from the waterfront. I walked back toward Main Street, the smell of diesel growing fainter as I moved away.

The Salty Dog wasn't actually on Main Street but halfway down a small lane that had one working streetlight at the other end of it. The Salty Dog had a wooden sign above the door that had a picture of a Border Collie on it. The sign was on iron rings and was creaking softly with the breeze. I pulled open a door made of oak planks and walked down into a bar that would have to do a lot of work to move up to being a dive bar. In the dim light, I was able to feel my way to a stool at the bar. The bartender was a fat man with a patch of thinning dark hair, a mean little mouth, and a chambray work shirt. A white apron was tied low around his ample gut, and he looked at me and then away, as if he hadn't seen much of anything. I sat, eating pretzels out of a cheap plastic bowl. He eventually realized that I hadn't made a mistake and that I wasn't going to go anywhere, so he waddled down to where I was sitting.

"Whaddayahwant." It came out so fast that I almost said, "Bless you."

"Whadda yah have on tap?" I couldn't say it as fast. He grunted and pointed a finger that looked like a sausage at the taps, which I had long since memorized.

"Pabst and a shot of Wild Turkey." It seemed like a good idea.

"Ain't got no Turkey, just Jack, Jim, and Old Crow."

"Yeah, you do, on the third shelf middle." He just grunted and turned away. It was like watching a battleship turn. Nothing happened quickly, but you didn't want to be in the way, either. He pulled the tap and poured me a mug of Pabst and then poured the bourbon into the shot glass. He then lumbered up to where I was sitting and slammed both down on the cigarette-burned bar without spilling a drop.

"Four fifty," he barked out from somewhere just above his jowls. I slid a five across the bar to him, and he lumbered away to get change. By the time he came back with it, the bourbon had burned its way down to my stomach, the beer was half gone, and my friend from lunch was sitting next to me. The bartender slapped my change on the bar with his meaty hand and turned to my companion.

"Whaddayah havin', Lenny?"

"Same as my friend here." Lenny nodded toward me.

"You want another?" He had warmed slightly toward me.

"Same again, and his is on me." He nodded, which was like watching the ocean, and turned away.

"I'm Andy." I stuck my hand out. Lenny crushed it in his.

"Lenny Wilcox, used to be Specialist Five L. Wilcox."

"I used to be Staff Sergeant Andy Roark . . . that was a lifetime or two ago." He smiled knowingly.

"Yeah, me too." The bartender slid two beers and two shots at us and took my empty mug with a sleight of hand that I didn't think he had in him. I slid a ten onto the bar, and the bartender nodded. Lenny raised his shot glass and turned to me.

"To absent friends."

"Absent friends."

We clinked glasses, and for the second time in an hour, the bourbon didn't burn any less on the way down than it did with the last one. The beer following it was cold, and I was sure that I wouldn't be feeling any pain.

"I got what you asked for." Lenny was looking at me with serious, hard eyes.

"Okay." He had something to say.

"The person who owns it now is the same as who owned it in 1968, but . . ." he trailed off.

"But what, Lenny?" He didn't seem comfortable anymore.

"You are looking for a guy who split on his little girl, right? Nothing else . . . nothing bad, no scams or nothing like that?"

"Lenny, my client is an adult now, but she wants, for whatever reason, to find the father who left her when she was a little girl. Nothing more or less than that." Lenny looked me in the eye for a few seconds.

"The box belongs to Ruth Silvia. She lives out on an old farm out of town heading toward P-town." He slid a piece of paper over to me. It had her address on it.

"Thanks, Lenny, I appreciate it." I did. "Who is she?"

"She's a painter. Lived out in her farmhouse as long as I can remember. I think she bought the place after World War II. Turned the barn into a studio. She's an odd one."

"Odd how?" I was curious.

"Oh, every town has one. You know, the crazy old lady or the reclusive old man. No phone, no electricity. Comes to town only to buy food and supplies, otherwise lives out on their own. She owns a huge chunk of the Cape. People been trying to get her to sell it for vacation homes, but she won't let go. She is just sitting on money." I hadn't heard Lenny speak so much at one time.

The bartender kept bringing drinks. We were both happy to keep it to just beer. Lenny and I swapped some war stories and drank more beer. We talked about the shitty way we were treated when we got home. Some hippy had tossed blood on him when he landed in Seattle . . . someone had spit on him. He just wanted to come home to the Cape and spend summers on the beach, drinking beer and chasing skirts. He told me he didn't go to the beach much because of the scars. He didn't chase skirts because he had found a nice girl and settled down. Like everyone I knew or met, he was just trying to get beyond the war. To pack it up and put it in some box in the attic, only to be opened when drunk or we heard of another army buddy who died too early. We drank and ate pretzels till nine, when Lenny had to go home to his wife and their kids. I paid the bartender and went out to retrieve the Karmann Ghia.

Chapter 7

A sensible man would have found a hotel room or gone back to Boston. Even a slightly drunk man would have gone back to Boston . . . but beer and bourbon on an empty stomach combined to help me not be sensible. In the Ghia, I found my road atlas for Massachusetts and the page I wanted. I followed the road out of Hyannis and away from the roads I knew as a tourist. I kept the Ghia carefully in the lines and noticed how the headlights cut through the dark night. The sky beyond my windshield seemed vast and dark.

I passed her mailbox twice in each direction before I figured out it was hers. I parked down the road from her mailbox and walked back to it. The sky was black with clouds, and the wind had come up. I turned the collar up on the trench coat. I could feel the weight of the Colt .32 under my arm, and it gave me an irrational sense of comfort. The things that I was afraid of didn't live in the rational world but in my memories. None of the bad dreams could be stopped with bullets.

I walked up the soft sand driveway. In the distance, I could hear traffic, but most of it was drowned out by the wind. I could hear the occasional gull but not much else. I could smell the smoke from a fire wafting toward me. The road was flanked on either side by scrub brush and the short pine trees that you find on the Cape and seemingly nowhere else. Half a mile through the soft sand, the road bent at a forty-five-degree angle and sloped uphill. A quarter of a mile after that, I saw the house. It was a small farmhouse that dated back to the days when Massachusetts was a colony and not a state. I could just make out in the darkness the shape of a barn. There were no lights in the yard, and we were too far from the road for the streetlights to reach this far. Now the sound of the surf pounding on the beach was distinct.

I stood by the edge of the driveway for a minute, listening, and then moved around to the front of the house. A couple of the windows were lit by soft light. I stood quietly listening for something, not sure of what, but something. The wind slowed and quieted, and off in the distance I could hear the faint barking of a dog.

The front door was flung open, and standing in it was a woman with long, wild gray hair wearing some shapeless black garment. In her gnarled, rootlike hands she held an old double-barreled shotgun. It was old enough to have hammers. She stared out at the night, and her eyes looked dead at me.

"I know you're out there." I didn't say anything but stayed still. I could hear my breathing, and even though I knew it was soft and low, it sounded like surf on the beach to my ears.

"I know you are out there . . . I can smell the drink and cigarettes on you, so might as well say something."

I wasn't sure of what to say, so I simply said, "Hello."

She brought the shotgun up, not all the way, but perceptibly.

"Who's that? Who's there?"

"My name is Andy Roark, I apologize for coming by late like this. I didn't mean to disturb you, ma'am." She turned her head so that one ear was toward me.

"What do you want with an old woman at almost ten o'clock at night, Andy Roark?"

"Well, ma'am, I am trying to find someone who I think you knew in 1968."

"Well, you'd better come in, then, and have a drink with an old lady and ask about 1968, then."

"Thank you." I walked across the few feet to the door, and she stepped aside, shotgun pointed at the floor, as I drew near. The door frame and the ceilings were low. The ceiling had exposed, dark wood beams with off-white plaster between them. The light inside was soft, and it took me a minute to realize it was the product of a series of oil lamps with large glass chimneys. The inside was clean but smelled of something like damp sheepdog.

"We'll sit in the kitchen, I think, by the fire. Perhaps a drink to help you warm up, Mr. Andy Roark, who is interested in 1968." Her hair was gray, shot through with rich brown, and I couldn't tell if it was curly or just unkempt. It was a wild tangled mess. She smelled like a French dockworker. She led me down a short hallway to the kitchen. As we passed down the narrow passage, I noticed that there were paintings on every wall. They were mostly oils and looked something like O'Keeffe's flowers and seascapes. I didn't much care for them, but they were clearly art.

The short, low hallway opened to a kitchen that was dimly lit by the low fire in the large hearth. I hadn't realized that I had been cold until I drew close to it. Across from the fire was a large table made of rough-hewn planks that had been stained a dark, rich caramel. On either side were two matching benches. The old woman went to the table and lit a hurricane lamp in the center of it.

"Sit down, Mr. Andy Roark, sit." She pointed a gnarled finger at the far bench. She then turned toward some cupboards on the far wall. I could barely make out a sink and a rooster-shaped hand pump. She placed the shotgun in the corner by the counter and then reached up into the cupboard for a couple of glasses and a bottle of Old Crow. When she turned back to me, she fixed my gaze with two milky, unseeing white eyes.

"A drink will warm you up." She cackled, actually cackled, like something out of a bad movie. "Then we'll talk about 1968, Mr. Andy Roark." She put down two glasses, mismatched highballs from what had clearly once been different and expensive sets. She poured a finger of the bourbon into each glass.

"Do you fancy ice or water? If you do, you're out of luck. We don't serve either in this bar." She pronounced her words with that accent in Massachusetts that is handed down by the nuns. Either is pronounced "eye-ther." She cackled again and took a healthy sip of her bourbon. I did the same and longed for the mellower burn of the Wild Turkey.

"Now, Mr. Andy Roark, where are you from?" The unseeing milky eyes never left my face.

"Boston." I usually just say Boston.

"I hear the South mixing with that Boston accent." She overpronounced "Boston" the way that people do when they make fun of how we talk.

"I spent some time in the service . . . they beat as much of a Southern accent into me as they could."

I could still hear Drill Sergeant Whitting to this day, with his thick, syrupy Southern drawl.

"Roark, y'all speak like some kind of Yankee asshole . . . pahk the cah in the yahd. Y'all got to learn to speak like a civilized human being and shit, instead of a Yankee faggot.

Y'all hear?" It wasn't until after graduation that someone
took pity on me and told me that he was originally from
Utica, New York, but that he had been in the South for so
long that he adopted their culture in all forms. Traitor.

"Oh, a man in uniform . . . yes, yes, neat creases in your
trousers and spit-shined shoes. Which service?" She waved
a gnarled hand in the air between our faces.

"I was in the army."

"Were you nervous in the service? Were you in Vet-
nom?" The last was a potshot at how LBJ said Vietnam. It
was something a lot of guys used to say. Now no one
talked about Vietnam unless it was a plot point in some
bad movie.

"Yes, ma'am, I was in Vietnam." Ten years after the fact
it still felt strange to admit it. It was like admitting you
had gone to the World Series but you weren't part of the
winning team.

"Were you in the thick of it, or were you one of those
men who never fired a shot in anger?" The milky-white
eyes looked at where she thought my face was. The Old
Crow burnt my throat, and I was running low on snappy
comebacks.

"No, ma'am, I was in the shit."

"Well, then, you should have another drink. On me."
She was smiling and her teeth were the color of a used
meerschaum pipe. She poured us each another Old Crow
without spilling a drop.

"What brings you to my doorstep on this stormy night?"

"It isn't stormy tonight." She seemed to have the quality
of hearing things that only she could hear.

"It will . . . it will storm." She had the certainty that
drunks and the crazy have.

"Maybe so . . ." The wind was picking up outside,
enough that you could hear the tall grass and scrub pines
moving in the wind.

"Well, Andy Roark from Boston, what brings you to my hearth, to sit at my boiling cauldron this night?"

"I am looking for a man named Charles Edgar Hammond. His daughter, who hasn't seen him since she was a little girl, has hired me to find him." I wasn't sure how much to say. It is always a guessing game. You want to spark interest and seem open, but you don't want to give everything away.

"What makes you think I know your Charles Edgar Hammond? Or that if I did, I would tell you anything?" She smiled as she said it, and I wondered if she had been pretty when she was younger.

"Well, for three months in 1968, the VA sent his checks to the mailbox that you have had since 1949. Now, that could be some sort of coincidence, but I don't think so." The fire was flickering, and the oil lamp seemed to flicker with it in some sort of dance.

"Do you remember 1968, Mr. Vet-Nom Roark?" I nodded and then remembered that she probably couldn't see it.

"Sure, I was around for that."

"So do I. So do I. 1968 was my last waltz at the ball, last dance, last dance . . ." Clearly the cogs in the machine were slipping a little. "In 1968, this was an artist commune. There were always twenty people in the house and another few in the barn. During the summer months, people would come and stay in tents. One year we even had people staying in an Indian teepee. Can you imagine such a thing on my lawn?"

"Are you telling me that you don't know or remember Charlie Hammond?"

"What I am telling you is that on a good day thirty or so people could be living here. No one introduced themselves politely like you. We drank and ate and smoked and fucked and dropped acid. I might have rolled around with any three men named Charlie and not known that much about them." Then she imitated me. "Good evening, ma'am, I am Andy Roark, one of the killer Boy Scouts. . . . I am looking for a ghost from years ago. . . . Do you know him? Andy Roark, many of the men I knew then I didn't talk to very much."

"Charlie Hammond received three months of VA checks at your mailbox?"

"Sure, he did. Everyone got mail at my mailbox. We had a blue '48 Ford pickup that they would take into town for mail call every day. They'd sort the mail and put it in a big metal box out front, and everyone would get their own."

"So, was Charlie Hammond here? It sounds like his mail was." I punctuated my question with some of the bourbon.

"I don't know. In 1968, while you were probably off killing little yellow men, the people here didn't use last names. It was all first names or nicknames or names they chose. I don't remember anyone named Charlie, but if he was here, he could have been Star or Wolf or Columbus or Bolivar or Che or Peace . . . that is just how it was. Not only that, but in 1968 we dropped a lot of acid . . . smoked a lot of grass and a lot of hash. I even had a few drinks. There were whole weeks that went by when I didn't wear a stitch of clothing. Even if I was concerned about the details, and I am not, I am pretty sure that I couldn't remember them." She leaned over and picked up a fire poker and started to stir the embers of the fire.

"So, it is possible that he could have been here?" I was hoping for an answer of some sort.

"Andy Roark from Boston by way of Vietnam and blood and war . . . Charlie Manson and Ho Chi Minh could have been here in 1968 . . . I just couldn't swear to it." Her milky eyes were unblinking on mine in the firelight. "Now, Andy Roark, I hate to kick you out on a stormy night like this, but I am not long for this world and want to sleep."

"Of course, thank you for the drink and the hospitality."

"Oh, I haven't done you any favors . . . you will chase ghosts and wrestle with ghosts, and I will sleep. Warm in my bed while you are caught in the rain . . . no, don't thank me, killer man." She started to cackle, and I knew it was time to leave. I took the trench coat, and with the Old Crow burning my throat and her laughter full in my ears, I made my way down the hall to the door.

I stepped out into the chilly, damp air and paused to tie the trench coat around my waist and light a cigarette. I felt a drop on my face and then another. I could still hear her laughter or her laughing, I wasn't sure. The moon was gone, I should have walked down the soft sand of the driveway instead of letting rain water pelt my face and put out my cigarette.

Instead of walking down the driveway, I circled around the house toward the barn. In Scooby-Doo the bad guys always kept secrets in the barn. The barn had two big doors at either end. What should have been old, rusty hinges appeared to be well oiled. I was about to pull the handles and look inside. I stopped; it took me a second to see it in the dark, but nestled at the top of the doors was a wire and contact. An alarm. I went to the various windows; they were dusty and hard to see through. They were all wired, too. They were the newest things on an old, decrepit barn, populated by rusty hardware and cobwebs. All the doors and windows were wired on the ground floor. I heard the creaking, and hanging down on the side away from the house was a rope. A rope hanging from a davit and pulley so that things could be moved in and out of the hayloft. The hayloft doors weren't fully closed.

I found an empty trash can on the side near the house. I quietly brought it around to the rope. It wasn't fun climbing up onto the trash can in the rain after so much whiskey. Trying to be quiet. Ruth's house looked dark, but I didn't want to take chances. My fingers just reached the bottom of the rope. I squatted down, on top of the trash can as best I could, then jumped up. I caught the rope in both hands. The rope was wet and I slipped a couple of times on the way up but always managed to stay on the rope. I pulled hand over hand until I could lock the rope between my feet. The doors were open enough for me to get one foot in and slowly by twisting my foot back and forth open them enough to slide between them. They were fairly loose on their tracks and I was inside in very short time.

I paused in the hayloft. My breath was coming out in clouds of steam, reminding me I was not twenty-one anymore. I could smell hay, old animal smells, horse shit, and dampness. I knew why people put alarms on their houses, they had nice stuff they didn't want stolen, but why an old barn way out on the Cape?

I let my eyes adjust to the dark. If I were a better or more prepared private eye, I would have carried a small flashlight instead of leaving it in my car. I moved carefully around the hayloft; they usually had ladders and a lack of railings. I found the ladder and slowly went down it, descending into the murky abyss below.

I paused at the bottom. I waited, listening. The army had taught us that. Get off the birds, into the wood line, and listen. Wait. Wait for the enemy to make a noise.

The storm went on outside. Rain beat against the barn and in the few times it slackened the pounding of surf was the bass back beat. Then a crack of lightning, sharp brushes on cymbals, lit up the barn. Then the thunder that could only be the snare drums. No footsteps. No running. No yelling. Just me and a storm in a barn.

I could see an old tractor at one end and bits of old farming implements. In the corners there was the usual trash that you would expect to find in an old barn, bits of tools, burlap sacks, old paint, tins with nails, all of it rusting in the damp, salty air of Cape Cod. There were bags of potting soil and bales of hay piled near the door. The place was cluttered at the front by the tractor, but to the rear it was open.

Then against one wall were a series of what looked like square bales. They were wrapped in heavy-gauge plastic. There were about half a dozen of them stacked up. I went over to where they were and started to run my hands over them. The plastic was damp and cold but was unyielding as to its contents. Finally, I took out my pocketknife and cut a small hole in the back of one. The smell, bittersweet, hit me immediately, marijuana. Weed. A lot of weed. She had at least a couple hundred pounds of it, wrapped up.

It made sense. She was close to the beach. She had the space to store it, move it in bulk. Either she was dealing it large scale or just holding it for someone. Either way she would need security. Her sensing me coming down the driveway was not ESP. There must have been an infrared sensor somewhere. I went back up the ladder and then down the rope. I put the trash can back against the house. It was still raining and the lightning was still flashing.

I made my way carefully down the driveway. The sensor was just on the other side of the barn, just far enough away from the house to give warning. I stepped around it. I didn't want her to think that I had been snooping. Or that I might know she was involved in drugs.

As I went down her soft sand driveway, the drops began to fall a little faster. I could see the men that I had been friends with, and I could see my dispatched enemies. The rain began to come down in sheets, and the lightning cracked, and every scrub pine was made sinister by the Old Crow and being tired. My hair was plastered to my head, and the trench coat could only stop so much rain. I slogged down the driveway with the ghosts. The weight of the Colt under my arm was comforting, if only as a talisman against my inner demons.

I made it to the Ghia. It was cold inside, but at least it was dry. The motor turned over on the second try, and the windshield wipers began to beat time like Art Blakey. I eased onto the road and slowly made my way back to the center of town and from there back to the ribbon of highway that would take me over the canal and back to Boston and my cold, lonely, half-filled flat.

The wind drove the rain hard at the Ghia, and when I went over the bridge across the canal, the wind blew the Ghia all over the bridge. The public radio station out of Boston was a mix of static and faint jazz. It didn't matter, because it was hard to hear over the rain beating against the roof of the Ghia. On the curves, the Ghia hydroplaned a little, and my having been drinking steadily since noon didn't help. The roads were mostly empty, save for a delivery truck or two.

I drove slowly through the dark, stormy night. The rain beat against the windscreen, and the wind shook the car, and I drove slowly along the highway back to Boston. I thought of the old lady in the house. She was crazy, or at least on the road to crazy. She had told me enough, assuming she was telling the truth, to tell me that Charlie Hammond could have been there in 1968. Hell, Ronald Reagan could have been there in 1968 for all she knew.

I made it back to Boston and to my apartment somehow. The driving was scary enough that I didn't start feeling tired until Milton. When I pulled off the highway and onto the back streets, it was still dark, but the early-morning people were moving around. The rain was steady, but not the downpour that had soaked me on the Cape. I pulled into my spot behind the apartment and pulled my weary self out of the Ghia.

When I got upstairs, the apartment was still half-empty. Leslie still wasn't there. The air inside was stale, and I was too tired to realize that had become familiar. I hung my trench coat on the back of one of the chairs at the kitchen table. I locked the door and kicked off my sodden shoes. There wasn't much to see in the rest of the apartment. I was too tired to sit with a book and a drink, or to sit and brood. Instead I went right to the bedroom. The Colt .32 went on the bedside table, and the clothes went in a damp heap on the floor. I was too tired to take my watch off; instead I crashed into the bed and crawled under the covers to get what rest there was left to have.

Chapter 8

I slept close to the surface. The type of sleep where you hear every noise outside, toss and turn and mash the pillow a hundred different ways. I was too tired and too drunk when I went to bed. The sky brightened too soon. I tossed and I turned too much and rolled over a lot. Sleep was never something that came easily to me, and that night, or what was left of it, was no exception.

In my bad dreams that night, Ruth Silvia was dressed up in black VC pajamas and a conical hat. She chased me across a rice paddy with a giant paintbrush and laughed at me with her maniacal cackle until she turned into a VC with an AK-47. At some point in time, I was hiding in the rice paddy while she hunted me. Then I was drowning in the shit-filled paddy water. Every time I tried to get out of the water, she would cackle and put one bare, calloused foot on my face and push me back under the water. I tossed and turned and fought with the covers and the sheets. I woke up after six fitful hours and had a headache to call the people at Guinness about.

The bathroom had a hot shower and an Alka-Seltzer. I

turned the water on as hot as I could take it, for as long as I could take it, and then turned it to cold. Later, I sat in the kitchen smoking an unfiltered Lucky and drinking a cup of black coffee. When I thought my stomach could take it, I made some toast and ate it as an experiment in holding my food down. When I was sure that I wasn't going to be sick, I decided that I could make my way out in the world.

Outside it was windy, and there was a steady drizzle. It wasn't as bad as the night before, but it was steadier and chillier. My trench coat was still damp, and in no time my shoes squelched with every step. I felt like Philip Marlowe or Humphrey Bogart. The Colt .32 was still under my arm, and walking down Commonwealth Avenue, I could have been in some spy movie set in Paris. Orange and brown leaves had fallen from the trees and were spread out on the sidewalk and the street. There were pumpkins everywhere, and Halloween decorations were showing in windows and doors. It was the type of day that made me want to sit in a wing chair by a warm fire, reading a book and having a cognac.

I made my way to the Boston Public Library, stopping at Brigham's only long enough for a cup of coffee to warm me. The John Hancock was all glass and steel and reflected, as it always does, the buildings and sky around it. Today everything looked gray and wet, typical fall in New England. Inside, I made my way to the research section and the microfilm machines.

The librarian grudgingly let me have the microfilms that I wanted and had me sign for a machine. She was probably a nice lady, but her profession demanded she run the microfilm with all the seriousness of a matron in a women's prison. After three hours, I had read through back issues of the *Cape Cod Times* going back to 1946. I didn't see Charles Edgar Hammond's name anywhere, and Ruth Silvia's name came up twice. Once was in 1968, when the police were investigating an accidental overdose out at her commune. A drifter unknown to most of the commune had OD'd on heroin and hadn't woken up from his trip. The drifter was only known as Angel. The other article was about Ruth's sister. In 1955, Ruth's sister, Louise Adler, had died in a car accident. Louise was a widow and apparently owned a pretty sizable chunk of Cape Cod. The property was left to Ruth as Louise's only living relative.

I gave the matron back her microfilms, and she looked at me as though I had taken out back issues of *Hustler* instead of the *Cape Cod Times*. I just smiled blandly and thanked her. If she only knew. I made my way to the front exit and out into the damp. I walked to Government Center and watched as people were ducking in and out of the rain. A riot of different-colored umbrellas bobbed up and down on the pavement ahead of me as I made my way to Government Center.

Government Center was the collection of architectural monstrosities that had replaced perfectly sensible and attractive buildings that housed local, state, and federal government offices in Boston. To say that Government Center was ugly was an understatement. It was simply a pile of concrete and brick boxes stacked up on top of each other surrounded by brick pavilions.

I found the office I wanted in the ugly building that I wanted. A twenty-dollar bill convinced the clerk to stay open a little later than the sign on the office said. The Registry of Deeds in the Commonwealth of Massachusetts is a simple enough idea. Each county has its own office that records the deeds; then microfilm copies are made and sent to a central office in Boston. The clerk at that central office agreed with me that it would be faster and more profitable for him to take fifty dollars and Ruth Silvia's name and print out all of the documents relating to her and her property. For another fifty, he also gave me the maps of the deeded plots on the Cape. I took my paper booty and headed outside.

I used some of the Swift money to pay for a cab back to my place, so that the papers wouldn't get soaked on the way home. The cabbie was old Boston Irish, but he didn't try and take me to my apartment by way of Logan. I didn't get too wet running from the cab up into my building.

Inside, my trench coat was on the back of a chair facing a wheezing radiator. I had spread the plot maps out and started looking over Ruth's holdings. Ruth owned a pretty good chunk of Cape Cod. Not so much that they would rename anything after her, and not so much that it looked big on the map. However, when you did the math and looked at the real-estate pricing, she was worth a tidy sum of money. It wasn't Swift Aeronautical rich . . . but Ruth Silvia was a long, long way from being a starving artist. Looking at the papers, I realized that Charles Edgar Hammond could be living on any one of almost two hundred square acres of Cape Cod.

I went to the living room and found a red felt tip pen. I started to outline her property boundaries. There was one plot that I couldn't find. It was a large area, but the number related to the deed wasn't anywhere on the map. It took me twenty minutes, but I found the answer at the bottom of the map, in a key. The key had two ranges of deed numbers. One set was on the map for Martha's Vineyard, and the other set was on the Nantucket deed map. Ruth's other plot was somewhere on Nantucket Island. Little wonder it didn't show up. Nantucket was thirty miles out to sea to the southeast of Cape Cod. I went to the phone and called Danny's secretary. After a little back and forth, he came to the phone.

"I think you should buy me a few beers and tell me how damned smart I am." I can be a little cocky sometimes.

"You found something?" He sounded excited.

"I think I have what is known in the profession as a clue."

"A clue?"

"Yes, in professional detective speak, it is an indicator or piece of evidence."

"I know what a clue is. I want to know what your clue is." He sounded a touch annoyed.

"How do you like the paintings of Georgia O'Keeffe?"

"I don't. Most of them look like ugly pictures of ugly pussy. Why, is your guy hiding in one?"

"Nope, but I think I may know where he is hiding."

"Where?" Danny was definitely impatient.

"Nope, you have to buy me several beers and tell me how fucking smart I am." I was enjoying it. Being cocky and having something figured out before Danny . . . I was absolutely enjoying it.

"Okay, the usual place at 6:15." He was as impatient to hear it as I was to tell him.

"Okay, see you there."

"Andy?"

"Yeah?"

"You're a prick. You know that, don't you?"

"I do, you shyster, I do."

Chapter 9

I put away my deed maps, deed information, and the yellow legal pad that I wrote my case notes on. I used a yellow legal pad and blue and red felt tip pens. Later, the notes would get typed up, and the maps, pictures, whatever information that I have, would be packaged into a case file. I will send one copy and keep the original. Most cases were not that complex. Infidelity or insurance fraud were usually a few pictures and a summary. This case would probably run a bit longer. I could now see why the Pinkerton men wrote out a version that looked like *War and Peace*.

I slipped the Colt .32 back under my arm, put on a blue sport coat over it and my damp trench coat over that. I changed my wet shoes for a pair of older loafers and would just have to face the weather. I went outside and was surprised to find that the wind and the rain had let up. That was Boston in the fall. I started briskly toward the bar. It wasn't far, but it seemed it, dodging the puddles and trying to avoid being splashed by passing cars.

Danny, of course, got there before me. He was wearing

a suit of soft gold and green plaid, with a design so fine that at a distance he looked to be wearing a solid, soft green suit. He looked up at me in the mirror as I stood in the doorway. I stopped only long enough to hang my coat on the coat rack by the door. The crowd was the same as always, men and women in business clothes . . . professionals, lawyers, and accountants. Beautiful men and women who made good money and kept regular hours.

I half danced, half shouldered my way through them to the bar. Danny leaned over and said something to the young-looking office drone sitting next to him, and the kid got up and moved away. It was the lawyer equivalent of a dog pissing on a hydrant. Danny slid a Löwenbräu and a pilsner glass across the bar to where he had been sitting.

"You're late." He said it as he pointed a finger at me around his glass of scotch. It was his signature move.

"I made progress." I picked up the bottle of beer and ignored the pilsner glass. It was an old battle in the war of Danny and his wife trying to make me suitable for polite company. I think they wanted me to pass for respectable at their dinner parties with the upwardly mobile set.

"Progress, as in, on the case?"

"As in, on the case. As in, I have managed to go where Pinkerton couldn't." I was feeling more than a little smug. The beer was cold and helped me feel physically better than I had all day.

"You mentioned something about a clue." He was looking me dead in the eye. I was glad that I had never had to be on the stand opposite him.

"I did. I did." I was enjoying drawing it out.

"Would you care to elaborate?" Even Danny had limits to his patience. "Because I am missing dinner with my wife and daughters, and my wife is noticing that after a number of meetings I come home smelling of scotch, cigarettes, and bar. So why don't you elaborate before my marriage is irreparably damaged."

"You're Catholic. Your marriage can't be damaged." I smiled. "I figured out who had the P.O. box that Charles Edgar Hammond got his checks sent to for three months in 1968."

"That doesn't seem that impressive. It certainly is not worth damaging my marriage over."

"You are right, that in and of itself wouldn't be." He knew when to wait and did so, looking at me and nursing his scotch. "The P.O. box was then and is still leased by a slightly crazy hippie artist named Ruth Silvia."

"Relevance?" Danny wasn't physically in court, but I didn't think his mind ever actually left it.

"For a time, Ruth Silvia ran a hippie artist commune. I spent the wee hours of this morning drinking cheap bourbon with her and talking about the wild, wild year of 1968. She says that it is possible that Hammond might have been there in '68."

"Possible? She isn't sure?" Cross-examining me gently.

"She described '68 and the commune as one long party, or more accurately, one long, drug-fueled orgy." Danny grunted, reminding me that he is Catholic enough to disapprove of the goings-on in 1968. "Lots of acid got dropped, lots of pills popped, lots of grass got smoked. Not only that, but most people there were using first names or names they chose, like Moon or Phoenix."

"What makes you think that Hammond was one of them?"

"Two things. One, she went out of her way to tell me at great length about how anyone could have been there using an assumed name, and she wasn't sure. She was steering well away from him or anyone definitively being there."

"I am not following you."

"How would you describe the climate toward the gᵒ ernment in 1968, toward the establishment?"

"Not good at all."

"Is it safe to say that someone getting checks from the VA at a hippie commune might actually draw attention? Silvia says they had a system where people went into town to get the mail and then it was left in a communal box." I was smiling now.

"You are postulating that those checks would stand out, draw attention?" He was smiling now, too. "That someone receiving a VA check, taking it out of a communal mailbox at a commune would stand out? Is that what you are implying?"

"Yep, VA checks on a hippie commune in 1968, I think those would stand out a lot."

"Do you have anything else?"

"Yes, an anonymous drifter named Angel died of a heroin overdose there in 1968, around the time that the checks stopped coming to the mailbox."

"You think that was Hammond?"

"No, I don't. I think if I was trying to lay low on a commune, an OD would bring attention that I wouldn't want. The police would show up. The coroner would show up. There would be a lot of questions and a lot of IDs being checked. People would be run for warrants, and the police would probably tear the place apart pretty good. If I was trying to stay off of the radar, then I definitely wouldn't feel comfortable."

"And you would leave?" Danny said it the way that the smart kid in class always does, asking the question when the question is really the answer.

"Yep, I think I would split in a hurry."

"Okay, so where is he? Las Vegas, LA, where?"

"Nantucket." This time I got to be the smart kid in class

instead of Danny. I smiled and ordered another Löwenbräu on Danny's tab. I looked up at the mirror behind the
bar and noticed the woman from before with the honey-
colored hair. Tonight, she was dressed conservatively in a
gray business suit. The skirt went down past her knees,
but she definitely had great calves. She had a brooch, but I
couldn't make out what it was other than shiny. The guy
with the perm was talking to her, and I wanted to believe
that she looked bored.

"Nantucket Island . . . off of the Cape?" Danny didn't
like curve balls.

"Yup, small island, shaped like a shoe. Former whaling
capital of the world, setting for *Moby Dick*. 'Call me Ishmael' and all that." I enjoyed being a little smug with
Danny.

"I am familiar with it. Why do you think he is there?"

"Ruth Silvia had a sister who died on Cape Cod in
1955. She owned a lot of the Cape, which Ruth inher-
ited." I was laying it out slowly for Danny.

"I still don't see it."

"I went to the Registry of Deeds to look up Ruth's land
holdings on the Cape . . . which are substantial." I explained to him how the deeds were recorded and tracked.
"There was one plot that I couldn't find on the map. It
was driving me nuts until I looked at the key."

"The plot is on Nantucket?" It did not take him long to
put the pieces together.

"The plot is smack in the middle of Nantucket." I said it
grinning at him.

"I think I should have had dinner at home." Danny was
not smiling.

"Why?" I pretended to be hurt.

"Because this isn't evidence, this isn't even a clue . . .
this is a hunch. At best, it is solid conjecture," he added.

"Danny, most detective work is a mix. The evidence runs cold on the West Coast in 1972. LA or Las Vegas. That is it." I was explaining it slowly.

"Yes." He was skeptical, and the economy of words was evidence that he didn't want to commit much more to my hunch.

"If you were looking to go to ground or just drop out of society, Nantucket is about as far from the West Coast as you can get. It gets a lot of tourists in the summer but is pretty slow and desolate in the winter. It is small enough that you will know if anyone comes looking for you, but big enough that you can stay out of the way."

"That is true." He was slowly warming to the idea.

"We know that he is connected to Ruth Silvia, we know she has land out there."

"It isn't much." He liked to throw cold water on my ideas.

"It is a lot more than anyone else has come up with. What if he is connected to her in other ways?" I held my hands up as though offering him something. An idea, a theory, something to take the case to the next step.

"What other ways?" Danny always liked to see the angles of his cases. He liked to see each one like a pool shark likes to know his table. That was part of what made him a great lawyer.

"The dead guy who OD'd might be one. Maybe there is more to it, or maybe Ruth Silvia was involved in some way?"

"Or maybe he just OD'd and she isn't involved at all." Danny was cross-examining.

"Or maybe he is a distant cousin of some sort? Or nephew?"

"Or maybe he isn't."

"Or maybe we just don't know what the answer actually is yet, but we will."

"Maybe." He sounded skeptical. The woman with honey-colored hair seemed to be bored with the guy with the perm. She was scanning the bar and the mirror. Our eyes met in the mirror, and she paused for a second, looking at me. She moved on. There was a better bet somewhere.

"Also, she's mixed up in something shady."

"How do you know?" He was zeroing in on me with his laser-like attention.

"I met her last night." I told him about the visit, the shotgun, the drinking. Then I told him about the barn, the pot, the alarms, etc.

"You think she's a big-time drug dealer?"

"Or she's working for one. She has the room, she has access to the ocean, why not?"

"So, what's next? A trip to Nantucket?" Danny's court voice brought me back to the bar, the case, and reality. Great-looking women with honey-colored hair and great calves don't go in for the likes of me.

"No, I want to look into the OD at the commune. I'll go and get the police report and see if I can talk to someone who was working as a cop at the time." It was the next logical step.

"What do you think that will tell you?" He followed his question with a belt of his scotch.

"I don't know. I just want to see if there is any more to it. I want to see if there was anything that didn't make it into the police report that might help me."

"Then Nantucket?" he asked.

"Probably, unless I find something that leads me in a different direction. You never know. Most cases are straightforward. If someone hires me to find out if their husband or wife is cheating, they already know. They are hiring me to confirm it. If an insurance company hires me to find out if someone is trying to defraud them, it is usually as simple as taking pictures of Johnny Chronic Back Pain working off the books as a furniture mover. Most missing persons cases are about finding runaway kids who run off with their boyfriend or girlfriend because Mom and Dad don't want them together. Most of the work I do is kind of boring. This is different."

"How is this different?"

"This is a puzzle, almost a mystery. This guy disappears for years and now, after the big shots have failed, we have a shot at figuring it out." I was feeling fine about myself. The woman with honey-colored hair got up and went to the ladies' room, and the guy with the perm just looked around, surveying the bar for another prospect.

"All right, I will concede that you might be on to something. Listen to me, Andy. This case could be important to me. This could open doors with the Swifts. It could mean a lot for me and my family."

"What, you want a new class of clients? Ones that aren't mobsters?"

"Exactly. That is exactly what I want. I don't just want to be a guest in the country club, I want a membership. I don't want to hear people whispering when I walk by their table in nice restaurants. Do you know what they call me? The Counselor of Cosa Nostra. I fucking hate that. Don't fuck this up for me, Andy!"

With that, Danny excused himself to go home to see his wife and kids. I stayed for another beer at the bar. Somehow, I had missed the woman with the honey-colored hair when she slipped out of the bar. She hadn't left with the guy with the perm, because he was down the bar from me hitting on a woman with big teeth who seemed responsive. I was slightly sad about the woman with honey-colored hair leaving. I was working up the nerve to ask her on a date. Perhaps dinner at the Café Budapest, Bull's Blood by the glass, fiddle players, and romance with a Hungarian accent. Maybe she liked detective novels, film noir, Bogart movies, strange cuisine, and lost causes . . . if so, I was probably the man for her. The odds didn't look good.

I left with my daydreams when I had finished my beer. I reclaimed my trench coat and hat, and stepped out into the chilly night. I stopped in the doorway long enough to light up a Lucky and then stepped out into the inky evening. It isn't that I thought I was being followed . . . I just wasn't sure that I wasn't being followed. It was still windy and wet, a classic nor'easter. I watched the cars drive by as I made my way home, their lights splashing along the buildings and pavement and sometimes on the happy couples walking by, arm in arm under an umbrella.

Someone had put a cardboard jack-o'-lantern and skeleton up on the door to the building. I let myself into the apartment and smelled the old tobacco of too many cigarettes smoked and not enough fresh air. I hung my trench coat by the hissing radiator and changed into an old pair of jeans and my BPD academy sweatshirt. The apartment was empty, and there was nothing good on the Movie Loft so I had no interest with whatever was on the TV. I turned on the radio to the public radio station that plays jazz every night after seven.

I poured a drink and stood near the window, looking out at the cars, sipping scotch, and smoking a cigarette. The headlights of the passing cars went by, their lights defying gravity and crawling up walls at impossible angles. The trees on the avenue were swaying back and forth like a couple of drunken dance contestants. Leaves fluttered by and spiraled down to the wet ground. I sipped my scotch and smoked my cigarette and was just as alone as when I had woken up. Charlie Parker was playing his saxophone music on the radio.

After a while, I opened a can of stew and put it on the

stove. After another glass of scotch had been poured and drunk slowly, I made some elbow pasta and drained it. The stew went on top, and it helped soak up the whiskey in my stomach. The dishes went in the sink, and I settled on the couch with more scotch, the Philip Marlowe stories, and the music of Chet Baker to keep me company until it was time to go to bed, where I fell asleep to the sounds of cars outside my window.

Chapter 10

Morning came with bright, brittle sunshine in my eyes and the radiator hissing in the corner. The storm had broken from the day before, and now the trees had lost many of their red and orange leaves. There were puddles everywhere reflecting the sun, and a few brave birds were around chirping. It was still windy out, but it wasn't blowing nearly as hard as it had been the day before. I made a pot of coffee and sat down with my notes and a cigarette. On my second cup of coffee, I switched from my notes to the clippings from the *Cape Cod News*. It was on my third cup that I reached for the phone and dialed Information. The nice lady at the other end gave me the phone number for the Barnstable Police Department.

I dialed and spoke to a very nice clerk. After assuring her that I was not a tourist looking for an accident report from the summer, I was able to get a word in edgewise. I explained that I was a licensed private investigator and that I was looking for information about an accidental death that had occurred in 1968. She asked the particulars of the case, and I explained about the OD out at the Silvia place. She said that she might be able to get me a copy of the report, and I told her that would be great. I also asked if I could set up an appointment to speak with someone who might have been working then. I was put on hold for five minutes; then she told me to be at the station at noon. I thanked her and hung up.

I showered and dressed in my usual jeans, white shirt, and corduroy jacket, with battered loafers. Leslie used to say that I looked more like a professor or grad student the way I dressed and with my long hair. After all the rain, I took the time to clean and oil the Colt .32 before slipping it under my arm in its usual place. My trench coat was mostly dry, and I found a pair of my old army-issue aviator sunglasses to combat the bright fall sun.

The Ghia took a few tries to start after all the heavy rain that had beaten its way under the hood over the last few nights. I made my way through the city traffic like a matador in the bull ring but finally broke through onto 3 South mostly unscathed. The trees were reddish orange, but the wind was stripping them slowly but surely of their leaves. In another week or two, they would be bare and sad looking. I followed the road through the hills and down toward the Cape, as I had a few days before. The drive wasn't any different, but I felt different. Things in the case were taking on a form, substance instead of being the dead-end file from Pinkerton. I actually had a lead to follow. I had, unlike a few days before, a sense of possibility.

Instead of classical music from the public radio station, I was listening to a station that went heavy on music by The Stones, Doors, The Who, and even some Pink Floyd. Now the Ghia and I were charging toward the Cape, buffeted by the wind left over from the nor'easter. I listened to the pounding drums of The Who and pushed the gas pedal closer to the floor. I rolled over the bridge that spanned the canal and made my way around the rotary. I followed the road that ran parallel to the canal and through the dense scrub brush by the air force base.

I imagined what wild country the Cape must have been when the Pilgrims first arrived. I could only picture how desolate and lonely it was. The spare and lean land in the winter was not well-suited to farming at the best of times. Would they have made it without the abundant fishing or the help of the Indians? I could almost picture it. Now it seemed that they were building houses and hotels any place that they could pack them in.

I turned onto Route 6, where the real spare, lean beauty of the Cape is on display. Tight bunches of scrub pine and bayberry lined the road. Here and there a cranberry bog slid into and out of view as the Ghia whizzed by. Gulls turned and wheeled overhead, sometimes lost against the sun or occasional cloud. I could see the tan of sand-covered roads, like Ruth Silvia's driveway, running off at odd, irregular angles.

I turned off of 6 and headed toward the airport. I went around another rotary and turned into town, all of it taking about ten minutes compared to the hour in traffic it had taken when Leslie and I had been here in the summer. I liked the Cape in the off-season. I liked the lean, windswept beauty of it. I liked it when it wasn't crowded.

The police station was one of those buildings that was designed by an architect who couldn't decide what style he wanted to choose from and settled on the worst of both. In this case, it was a mix of redbrick meets Cape Cod clapboard. The brick was too red, and the clapboard had been painted too white. A single blue and white Ford prowl car with its bubble light was parked in front of a sign that specifically forbade parking in front of it. The parking lot had two unremarkable cars in it, and I added the Ghia to the lot and walked into the police station.

I went in through the double doors that looked more

like they belonged on a bank than a police station. Across
from the doors was a counter with thick glass, behind which
sat a woman with curly brown hair, smoking a long, thin
cigarette. She was on the phone with someone and motioned me to sit in the blue, hard plastic chairs across from
her window. On the wall was a poster that showed an apple
with something in it encouraging parents to go through
their kids' Halloween candy.

I sat for five minutes, smoking a cigarette of my own
until she hung up and motioned me over. I slid the photostat of my license through the small opening in the glass
and told her that I had an appointment. She looked at the
photostat and then at me. She slid it back to me and told
me to sit down again. I passed the ten minutes by looking
at the wanted posters and posters on the walls about drug
use and teenage drinking. A door opened to my left, and
there was a tall, bald man in a white shirt and gold badge,
with major's oak leaves on his collar. He had a stainless-
steel, large-frame revolver, a Magnum of some sort, in a
hand-tooled leather holster on his Sam Browne belt.

"Mr. Roark?" I stood up and he stuck his hand out.
"I'm Deputy Chief Phil Blount." His hand was big and
raw-boned and swallowed mine. My hand throbbed, only
slightly, after he had released it. "Come this way."

He led me through the door and through a room with a
few desks and typewriters for the patrol officers to do their
reports. Past that was a room with a camera and finger-
print station, and a door that probably led to the cell
block. Blount led me back into an office with a big metal
desk—calling it ugly was an act of charity—and a couple
of chairs that didn't look inviting. One wall had a bookshelf with law books and the criminal codes. The walls
had pictures of a younger Blount in an army uniform with
a steel pot helmet and an M-14, and pictures of him at var-

ious ages and points of his police career. There was a window behind his desk with a view of some buildings. There were framed photos on his desk, family photos of him, a wife, and three normal-looking children. Wholesome. All-American.

"How can we help you today, Mr. Roark? What has brought you all the way down here from Boston?" He smiled at me with a long-practiced smile that all cops have, the type that isn't friendly or warm or anything. Just teeth and guarded intent, a smile in name only.

"I am looking for information about an OD that happened out here at a hippie commune in 1967 or 1968? The commune belongs to a woman named Ruth Silvia." His face didn't darken or change, but it didn't warm up to me, either. Dark, cold eyes and pale English skin with an old scar on the jaw were looking back at me.

"What is this about?"

"It might have something to do with a case that I am working on. Or it could be nothing, but I have to check it out." I smiled at him as best I could. He probably didn't like what he saw. A guy dressed in clothes that were too far from a uniform, with sandy hair that was too long and a beard that wasn't quite neat enough.

"What is the case?"

"It is a missing person case. Like I said, the OD is probably not related, but I wouldn't be doing my job if I didn't look at all of the angles for my client." His eyes stared at me with the professional flatness that cops have.

"Who is your client?" He smiled almost genuinely, like a little kid with a magnifying glass over an anthill. In the detective movies and books, this is the point where I would tell him that I can't tell him who my client is. If this were a forties detective novel, he would hit me with a sap or call in one of the boys to work me over before running me out of town. Fortunately, there wasn't much noir going around in 1982.

"I was hired by a Boston law firm to find a man named Charles Hammond." I told him the name of Danny's firm, but that was it. He looked at me, and I expected to be told to hit the bricks.

"The only two guys that I can think of who were working it are retired in Florida or dead. Pretty much the same thing."

"I was pretty sure it was a long shot. I appreciate your taking the time to meet with me." I started to get up.

"There was a guy on scene. It wasn't his call, but he was there helping out." I sat back down.

"I don't suppose he is still alive and not living in Timbuktu?"

"He lives here in town. Let me give him a call and see if he will meet with you." Blount picked up the phone on his desk and pushed some buttons from memory. He listened, looking at me, and then half turned away.

"Web, Phil Blount, how you doing? Good, thanks. Nope, she's just fine . . . kids too. Good, glad to hear it. Listen, I got a fella in my office who came all the way from Boston to ask about an OD that happened out at the Silvia place in '67 or '68. Uh-huh . . . yeah, it was a long time ago. Nope, I wasn't working here then. Yep. You think you could spare a few minutes to talk to this guy? Nope, used to be, private license now. Seems okay. All right, I'll send him out your way." Blount hung up the phone and turned back to me.

"Web will meet with you at his place. I'll give you directions. Web is kind of old-fashioned, so he might seem a little standoffish at first. Don't let it throw you." Blount actually smiled.

"No problem. I am sure the last thing he wants is a long

hair on his front steps." I pointed to the picture of Blount in the army uniform with the rifle and the Airborne patch.

"Yeah, I got out in 1962. I finished out my tour and ended up out here and became a cop." He smiled again and then said, "Let me write out directions for you to Web's house." He picked up a pen and paper and jotted down directions.

I didn't bother mentioning that I had been in the army, or that if I hadn't been where I was, I would have ended up in the Airborne. I didn't mention it because he would have done the math in his head and asked about Vietnam. Nobody wanted to talk about that anymore. Everyone just wanted to act like nothing had happened. No war, no protests, no . . . nothing. America was like a family at a holiday dinner that just got over a big fight and was pretending that it hadn't happened, that everything was normal.

Blount explained the directions to me, wished me luck, and stuck out his hand. He crushed my bones again and then showed me out. I walked back out into the fall sunshine and the sounds of the gulls wheeling overhead. The Ghia was where I had left her, a princess among paupers.

Chapter 11

The ride through town was short enough, even with my making a couple of wrong turns and having to work around some one-way streets. I ended up on a small, quiet street on the other side of The Steamship Authority. I pulled the Ghia in front of a small white clapboard Cape, with a small front yard and water view. I parked and walked up the steps. The front door was the same shade of blue that the ocean was on a calm day. The door itself was flanked by brass port and starboard running lights. My knock on the unremarkable blue door was met by a tall, stooped man with slicked-back gray hair and watery blue eyes.

"Mr. Webster?" He nodded. "I'm Andy Roark . . . Deputy Chief Blount said I should talk to you." I left it at that. He looked me over, and I, in turn, saw a man who was once physically powerful but whose body was betraying him with its age. His hands were big, with tobacco stains on his thumb and index finger, and his face was ruddy. He had the small starburst of veins in his nose and cheeks that comes from a lifetime of too much drinking.

"Call me Web. Only the damned Jehovahs call me Mr. Webster." He stuck his hand out and we shook. "C'mon in." I followed him inside. On one side was a table, and to the right I could see a couch and a TV in another room that seemed to run perpendicular to the one I was standing in. In front of me was a kitchen. All of it was done in knotty pinewood paneling. Not the fake laminate, but real pine boards, lovingly fitted tongue and groove, stained the color of good single malt scotch. All of the artwork was nautical in one way or another. Seascapes in dark oils on the walls, a sailor's valentine in the corner, bits of driftwood that had been turned into lamps, braided rope for frames or around colored glass lamps—it was all there. There wasn't a feminine touch anywhere that I could see.

"This way." He led me around to the room on the right, which was low and long, taking up half of the first floor. There was a stairway off to the left leading upstairs, and old Persian rugs covered the floors. The room had two couches, two chairs, and a big console TV. I followed Web to a door at the far end of the room and into an enclosed sunroom.

"I don't get to sit out here once it gets cold, so I spend as much time out here as I can." He pointed me to one of the two leather wing chairs that were backed up against the house and flanking a small bookcase. There was a glass of amber fluid with a couple of ice cubes in it, sweating slowly on top of the bookcase. The top of the bookcase was covered with numerous concentric circles, where other glasses of scotch on the rocks had sat time and again over the years.

"Phil Blount said that you were interested in an OD out at the Silvia place?" It was a question any way you put it. The porch had the same nice paneling as the inside of the rest of the first floor. The windows were screened and were made up of a series of glass panels that opened outward at the bottom of each panel. The view outside of them was of the harbor, where the ferry would leave for Nantucket. I could see the occasional fishing boat going by.

"I am. I am working a missing person case, and I think that the subject may have been at the Silvia place around that time." I settled into my chair with the view of the harbor.

"I worked that case. It was kind of a dead end. Kid took too much H and didn't wake up. Not much to it." He was looking at me.

"I understand. Do you mind looking at a picture and seeing if you recognize the person in it?" He was packing a pipe with Captain Black and looked up at me with his watery eyes.

"Sure, you came all this way." He put the pipe in his mouth, lit it, and drew on it until it was going. The rich smell of pipe tobacco quickly filled the room. I pulled the picture of Charlie Hammond out of my pocket and handed it to Web.

"Does this man look familiar? By the time of the OD, fifteen years would have passed." Web held it up in the light and squinted at it. He puffed on his pipe, unleashing thick, rich clouds of smoke.

"I wish I could say for certain, but I can't." He shrugged and handed the picture back to me. He reached over and took a sip from his glass. "I know I didn't see anyone with short hair and pressed clothes. I wish I could be more help, but between the age difference and the hair, I just can't say."

"I understand. Who did you see there?" I slid the picture back in my pocket.

"Well, Ruth Silvia was there. She was different then. She had this spark. She was the type of woman who didn't give a damn about what people thought of her. She was older, but men, even men ten, fifteen years her junior, chased after her. Ruth was the type of woman that the good churchgoing women talk about in loud whispers after services on Sundays. That woman seemed like pure, carnal sin on legs. She'd look at you and suddenly you had an itch you needed to scratch.

"There was always talk that her place was like Sodom and Gomorrah. Every night there were parties, some said orgies, and if the wind was blowing right, you could smell the pot smoke from the road. We got called out there once in a while, but nothing came of it. Whatever was going on there was never enough to get us interested in it. In the winter, the place quieted down." He took a sip and pulled on the pipe and seemed to be in the memory of it inside the confines of his own head.

"Was there more to it, or was it just talk?" I didn't want the flow of memories to dry up.

"Oh, there was plenty to it. I don't know if they had full-blown orgies, but they definitely were into Free Love. There were plenty of drugs. Pot, pills, acid—that sort of thing. Hell, they kept a package store in town in business for two or three years by making weekly runs in that blue pickup truck of hers."

"Any real trouble before the OD?"

He turned a watery eye to me, looking at me over the smoldering bowl of his pipe like he was aiming a rifle at me.

"Nope, no real trouble. Occasionally someone would get drunk in town or one of the locals might get in a fight with one of the hippies, but that was about it. Mostly they liked to stay out at the farm and smoke, drink, and fuck." He turned to look out at the water.

"Did they make much art or sell much?" I wasn't sure of where I was going, I just didn't want to lose him.

"Art . . ." He coughed or maybe laughed. "The only one of them with any damned talent was Ruth. Have you seen her paintings?" I shook my head. "She was like New England's version of Georgia O'Keeffe. Rest of them were just there for the free ride and the good times."

"What were they like?" He was drifting a little and staring out the window.

"They were hippies, mostly middle-class kids. College kids, the types who thought that burning draft cards and marching around meant something, but they couldn't be bothered to actually get out and do it. Instead they drank and smoked and fucked. I think that Ruth liked to have them around so that she could feel like their mother. Or their prophet or something. She definitely didn't mind having beautiful boys around."

"They didn't have a lot of get up and go, then?" Web just snorted. "Who did the maintenance around the place? Did Ruth hire someone from in town?"

"Dunno, I always thought that she was happy to let the place fall down around her ears, but when we were out there for the OD, the place looked pretty good. Someone had definitely been taking care of it." He stared off at some unseen memory and sipped more of his drink.

"Someone from in town? A handyman?" I asked the obvious question.

"Nope, people in town didn't like Ruth. No wife would let her husband go out there to work. They were all afraid that Ruth would use her feminine wiles on their husbands." He all but snorted it at me.

"You said that they were into pot, pills, and acid? I saw in the report that the kid who OD'd did it on heroin. Did that strike you as odd? Was there anyone else there doing it?"

"No, heroin wasn't really big out here." He took a sip of his scotch and pulled on the pipe.

"How come the body of the OD was never ID'd? Even in 1968, they had teletypes and missing persons bulletins."

"Kid didn't have any identification on him. There were no flyers or bulletins matching his description. Kid didn't even have much in the way of personal effects. His old grungy clothes, Mao's *Little Red Book*, a small amount of H, and his works. That was it, all of it in an army surplus duffel bag. No jewelry except a shitty rope bracelet like you can get in the shops in town. The kid was just a blank. No one was even sure of his name. No one was going to look really closely at an OD. No tattoos and no scars, he was just generic, like an extra in a movie."

"He just appeared out of nowhere, didn't stay long, and died at Ruth Silvia's place?"

His head started to nod, moving toward his chest, and eventually staying there. He answered the rest of my questions by snoring at me for five minutes. I stood up to go, and his pipe fell out of his mouth and he woke up.

"Was I out for long?" His voice was thick with sleep.

"No, Web. I was just letting myself out. Thank you for your time."

"Sure, sure, sorry I couldn't tell you more."

"No problem. Thanks again."

He pointed to my chest with one thick, stained finger and said, "You ought to get rid of that thing."

"Excuse me?"

"That little Colt .32 popgun. You'll just get yourself hurt with something that small."

"Thanks." No one ever likes having their gun criticized.

"Seriously, get a gun you can put a man down with. At least a .38." He then laughed or coughed, and I was not sure which. I heard it rattling in his chest as I made my way through the house. The last thing I heard was the gentle, bell-like tinkling of ice cubes in his glass.

Chapter 12

I let myself out of his house and sought comfort in the Ghia. It was late afternoon, and if I left now, I would be in time to sit in traffic outside of the city and feel frustrated. Instead, I started the Ghia and headed for a restaurant near The Steamship Authority. It sat on a hill and overlooked the Steamship terminal and the dock. When a ferry wasn't in, there was a pretty good view of the water. It was the type of tourist trap that was decorated in lobster pots, fish nets, and nautical items, and counted on being close to the ferry to provide business.

The waitresses all wore tight shirts with horizontal blue and white stripes and little black captain's hats. The drinks came with a lot of ice and a little bit of booze, and the cocktail napkins had red lobsters in the corner. The menu featured every possible variation of deep-fried seafood in the Western world, as long as you wanted fried clams, fried shrimp, fried scallops, fried oysters, fried haddock, fried cod, or fish and chips. They also offered clam cakes, but everyone knows that the best clam cakes come from a small clam shack in Narragansett, Rhode Island, named after somebody's aunt. Tonight, they also had a lobster roll on the menu as the special. It is a well-known fact among the three or four people who know me that I am trying to become the world's leading authority on lobster rolls and eat them almost whenever they are offered.

I sat at a small table with a green tablecloth and candle in a red glass holder. I had a view of the harbor and could see the bright sun begin to ebb across the last bit of blue sky. The waitress with blue and white stripes stretched tight across her ample breasts brought me a Cutty Sark on the rocks. There was just enough whiskey in the glass to moisten the ice cubes. I ordered a lobster roll with a side of coleslaw. When in Rome and all that. The Cutty tasted harsh and good all at once. That first sip of whiskey is always a mixture of iodine and astringent, but when the ice starts to melt, the flavor and sweetness of the whiskey opens up. After the first few sips, I felt warm and less tense.

I had a yellow legal pad on the table in front of me and was trying to make sense of what I had just learned. Had I just learned anything? In the 1960s, it was common knowledge that Ruth Silvia had a commune of sorts. Mostly a drug-fueled orgy out of which only she seemed to produce art. According to Web, most of the people who were there were privileged losers, the types who could afford to drop out of society and drink and smoke and screw. They mostly kept to themselves and went into town when they had to.

According to Web, they weren't into hard drugs, so where did John Doe get his heroin? How come the kid didn't have any ID? If the people at Ruth's were as ambitionless as Web said, who was doing the maintenance on the place? The waitress came and saw me scribbling on the pad.

"You want another drink, hon?" Her accent was what could be charitably called local.

"Please, a double this time?" I had to compensate for the unfair ratio of ice to scotch.

"Sure. What are you doing, work?" Her voice wasn't as bad as the sound of the gulls.

"Something like that." I smiled at her, but it was as good as their ice with a trickle of scotch cocktails.

"What are you, a professor or something?" She was chewing a piece of gum with an aggressiveness that reminded me of a police dog going at someone's leg.

"No, I write children's books." My smile was starting to hurt my face.

"Oh, huh . . ." She did an about-face and walked away.

She came back with my lobster roll, coleslaw, and scotch. She set them down in front of me and left without asking if I wanted anything else. The lobster roll was served right, tons of meat and enough, but not too much, mayo, heaping out of a buttered, grilled hot dog bun. I finished the meal fairly quickly. I decided to have one more scotch and watch the lights of the darkened harbor. I didn't have much more to add to the legal pad and couldn't eat any more if I had wanted to. I paid and tipped her more than she deserved, but the lobster roll was good.

In the Ghia, cutting through the dark night, I felt full and warm. Life wasn't bad. I was listening to jazz on the radio and smoking Luckies. The Ghia hummed up the road, and I was impressed as I always was when the night sky started to get purplish; then the skyline of the city loomed, well-lit, in front of me. I could see the Prudential and the John Hancock towering above the rest of downtown. I took the off-ramp and started making my way through the maze of one-way streets that define driving in Boston.

It took a little bit longer because the streets were full of half-sized cowboys, ghosts, Stormtroopers, and princesses. The other assorted pint-sized professions were represented, too. They moved about in slow-moving packs, wielding flashlights and carrying pillow cases. It made for slow driving.

My parking spot in the back of the building was more or less the same as I remembered it. I parked and got out. I could hear little kids moving in the streets. In the alley behind my building it was dark. The light on the side of the building was out. Either burned out or enterprising thieves had preemptively smashed it as they had done in the past. Sometimes the light just went out until it felt like coming on again. I could hear someone shuffling in the dark.

My eyes weren't adjusted fully to the dark. There were inkier pools of it farther back in the alleyway. I pushed, rather than slammed, the car door shut. I heard a muffled cough in the darkness. Someone was there. I stepped deeper into the darkness away from my car. I was feeling my way against a low iron fence, on the other side were trash cans. I could hear breathing. Was someone waiting for me in the dark? I started to sweat, as my hand, with a mind of its own, snaked into my jacket and pulled out the Colt .32. I tried to take the safety off quietly, but it sounded like a sledgehammer on pavement to me.

I could hear his breathing. He wasn't far. I could hear the rustle of clothing. Then the Arc Sodium light kicked on and I was staring at Death. Black robes, scythe, skull for a face. I almost put two bullets into the skull.

"Hey, man!" Aggrieved. "Hey, I just came back here to get sick. I had too much to drink. I'm sorry. Please don't shoot me." He was a college kid. Just a fucking kid whom I had almost shot in the face.

"Screw." I waved the pistol as my hand began to shake. The kid didn't need to be told twice.

I let myself inside the building and away from the cool

fall weather. Upstairs and inside the apartment, nothing had changed. There were no messages on the machine. There were only half the books, records, dishes, and furniture. There was no Leslie, no woman with the honey-colored hair, not even a buxom waitress in a silly sailor's outfit. I had no plants and, unless you counted the dust bunnies under the furniture, I had no pets.

Maybe I should get a cat or something to keep me company. Instead, I settled for jazz on the radio, scotch with ice in a glass, and more detective stories on the couch. I couldn't see myself with a cat. I have nothing against them, but I just couldn't see one sitting on my lap while I read.

I woke up the next morning when the rude man with the jackhammer started to tear up the sidewalk. I rolled over and tried to pull the pillow around my head, but the man with the jackhammer was a professional, and I had to give in and get up. There was nothing left to eat in the house, and the jackhammer was making life less than bearable. I showered, dressed, and decided on breakfast out at the greasy spoon around the corner.

It was sunny out but chilly, and I was glad to have remembered the scarf I was wearing. People were starting to wear scarves and gloves when they were out. You could see your breath as you walked, but it still was chilly only in the morning and night. Empty candy wrappers fluttered by, reminding me of last night's packs of marauding midgets.

I thought about the kid in the alley. I had almost shot him. It wouldn't have taken much. Was I cracking up? Leslie always wanted me to go talk to someone. She was worried about my dreams about the war. Was it catching up with me? Was I imagining the NVA, the Cong in my parking lot now? Was I reacting and thinking like I was back in Vietnam? Back on the trail? How the fuck could I function like that? Even I knew that pulling a gun on a drunk college kid was not an appropriate way to act here.

On the way to the greasy spoon, I stopped to buy a *Globe* and a pack of Luckies. I stepped into the greasy spoon and sat at a free seat at the counter. I went there often enough that the waitress didn't have to ask me if I wanted coffee. I ordered a cheese omelet, potatoes, bacon, and toast. I read the paper until she brought the food. It was all depressing, and I was glad when I was able to eat and not worry about the state of affairs in the world or in the Commonwealth. I paid and left.

Back in my apartment, I spent the rest of the morning making phone calls and travel arrangements. I set up a reservation on the ferry to take the Ghia and myself out to Nantucket. Next came a call to a hotel that I remembered in town. It wasn't far from the ferry, and it was nice and clean. I couldn't afford it in the summer, but in the off-season it was reasonable enough. It certainly wouldn't raise eyebrows on the expense account. I called Danny's office to talk to him, but he was in a conference, so I just left a message with his secretary about my going to the island in the morning and where I would be staying.

I was still working through *The Raymond Chandler Omnibus* but wanted something else to read. I went out and walked the many blocks to the Brattle Book Shop. I have been known to spend almost as much time in there as I do in bars. It is dark and quiet and has books floor to ceiling on two floors. The Brattle Book Shop is the closest thing that I have to a church.

I started in History and made my way to Political Science, strolled through Literature, and made a brief tour through Poetry. I picked up a copy of *The War with Hannibal* by Livy and a translation of Jean Lartéguy's excellent

The Centurions. By the time I left the store, I had the book about Hannibal, *The Centurions*, and two detective stories by James Crumley.

I started the walk back with my bag of books and was enjoying the nice afternoon weather. Once I thought I caught sight of honey-colored hair, but that must have been my wishful thinking. I stopped into Brigham's for a cheeseburger and coffee milkshake, as much to rest and have a bite as to look at my new purchases. I sat at the counter. The lunchtime crowd was back at work, and my company was comprised of a couple of senior citizens, a junkie sleeping in a booth for two that no one wanted to go near to wake up and kick out, and a whore and her pimp.

The junkie slept in his booth, moaning and stinking and generally being a mess. The pimp and whore were talking about catching a bus back to Providence, Rhode Island. The old people ignored us all in favor of their sepia-tinted memories. The waitress brought my food, took my plate, and took my money, all in that order. This was life in Brigham's on the edge of the Combat Zone, not far from the bus station.

I walked back home, mentally making and rejecting the list of things that I had to pack for my trip. I made lists of people I would try to see and questions I would try to ask. I was pretty sure that nothing would actually work out the way I planned in my head. At least I had some good books to take with me.

Chapter 13

The Ghia was gliding down the highway in what was now an all-too-familiar trip to the Cape. I had the engine opened up wide, and it felt like we were flying down the road. I was listening to Steely Dan on the radio and tapping my fingers on the steering wheel with the beat. The sun was playing tag with the clouds, but for New England in the fall, it was as good as you could hope for weather-wise. The Ghia shuddered as it bumped its way over the occasional pothole, frost heave, or expansion joint in the highway. It reminded me of being on a jump as the plane would shudder over turbulence. The Ghia clung to the curves and ate up the highway.

I pulled into the ferry parking lot with a good half an hour to spare. At the office, they took my money and told me where to park and wait. I, like a good troop, did what I was told. Anyone who has ever been in the army knows about waiting. While parked, I could see the sign for the restaurant I had eaten at a couple of nights before, poking over the roof of the ferry office.

I watched the ferry as it disgorged foot passengers from

the large, gaping maw of its car deck. After the people walked off, the cars and trucks leaving the island trickled out. In the summer, the process was long and tedious to watch. Now, sitting in the parking lot watching, it didn't take nearly as long. In no time, it was my turn to start the car and ease it up the metal ramp into the car deck of the ship. I wedged the Ghia between a Scout and the bulkhead of the ship.

I rummaged in my bag for a Jim Crumley novel and put it in the pocket of my jacket. I locked the Ghia and headed up the stairs to the passenger deck. This boat was named for the island to which it sailed and was large enough to carry cars and trucks. There was passenger seating in two bays along the port and starboard sides. The snack bar was centered on the top deck, with a stairwell on each side leading down to the passenger decks and then down to the car deck. The bridge was above the snack bar, but you never saw any of that. There were plenty of seats up in the snack bar, and that is where I headed with my Crumley novel. On an impulse, I went outside to look at the view and watch the world around the ferry as it bustled.

I could see people rushing to catch the ferry and cars driving by on the roads nearby. In the harbor, the occasional fishing boat steamed in one direction or another. At the appointed time, they cast off, and the ferry eased out of its slip. I could smell salt air and diesel fumes, and lit up a Lucky as my offering to the stew. We slid slowly past the docks and the boats tied up in their slips. At this time of year, there weren't that many moored in the harbor. We picked up speed, and the land started to widen and fall away on both sides. The wind picked up, and we slid farther out, and I decided that I would be happier in the snack bar.

The snack bar had coffee—it was too early for beer—

and chili, which was pretty good if you broke up some
Saltines into it. I sat in the snack bar eating my chili,
drinking my coffee, and reading my Crumley novel. It was
about a private detective with a past, and I liked it. Once in
a while, I would go out for a cigarette as the mood struck
me. As we moved farther from land, the swells picked up,
and the ferry rocked noticeably. It wasn't bad, but it was
enough to remind you that you were well out of the harbor
and away from land. We had pulled away from the mainland and were at the point where you couldn't see the
mainland, and you couldn't see the island, either. It was
the midway point that offered just a brief glimpse of what
it must be like to be a sailor. I knew it wasn't any sort of
life for me.

I went outside when the Nantucket headlands hove into
view. It was a sight to see, as the sun set over the headlands. I could make out the lights of the TV towers and the
faint outline of the water tower. Smoking a Lucky up on
the deck and watching the island come into view, I felt like
Bogart in some movie where he is jaded, romantic, cynical,
and, overall, decent. I was thankful for the nylon parka
from L.L. Bean. It was a faded blue with a thin plaid wool
liner and had big, roomy pockets. It reminded me of a
lighter, better version of the old M-65 field jacket that
every vet seemed to wear in order to let the world know
who they were.

Here and there lights twinkled in the houses near shore,
and headlights slid over the island in different directions.
As we moved closer, I could hear the bells on the buoys
and make out the faint outline of the jetties, which reached
out like a lover's welcoming arms to the ships seeking shelter in the harbor. Far off on the port side, I could make out
Great Point Light, to my front I could just see the rotating
spotlight from the airport playing along the low clouds,

and to starboard we passed Brant Point Light. We rounded
the point and made a hard-starboard turn. The harbor lay
before us. A few older sailboats, their days as the pride of
the fleet went on their way with the Kennedy administration, were now berthed in slips that they couldn't afford in
summer. Fishing boats now had the best spots in the ma-
rina, and the expensive yachts had moved to warmer, gen-
tler waters for the winter. It wasn't only the birds that
migrated seasonally around here.

In front of us I could see two different white clapboard
churches, their steeples lit by ground lights pointing up to
heaven. The terminal was made up of two buildings, both
were gray shingled with battleship gray painted trim. They
looked battered and in need of relief. One was a small
ticket office with some lockers, and the other was a long
gray shed that was designed to shelter people and steamer
trunks from the island's often cruel weather. Now it just
served to protect some cargo and passengers from the rain
and snow. I made my way down to the car as we slid in between the first set of wooden bumpers. They resembled
giant Lincoln Logs, bound together, forming some sort of
wooden teepee.

After a few minutes, cars started to turn over their engines, and I did the same with the Ghia. Cars started to
ease off of the ferry, and eventually it was my turn. I pulled
off the ferry and drove through the parking lot. My hotel
was literally three blocks away up Broad Street. The hotel
was a three-story brick building that was built before the
Civil War. When Leslie and I had come out to the island
before, it was summer and we couldn't afford to stay
there, much less get a reservation. However, this was the
off-season, and a reservation was not a problem. Mrs.
Swift's generosity meant that cost wasn't a problem. I
parked out front and walked up the stone steps and into

the hotel. I had my canvas postman's bag with me and must have looked a little bit like a bum. The woman at the counter looked as though she thought I had walked into the wrong establishment.

I explained that I had a reservation and paid the deposit on the room with Mrs. Swift's crisp one-hundred-dollar bills. The nice lady reluctantly gave me a key and told me I could park the Ghia in the lot behind the hotel. She seemed relieved when I told her I didn't need the porter's services. I took my bag up to the room and was pleased to find a small, neat, comfortable room with a bed, desk, TV, and bathroom. The room was furnished with elegant colonial pieces that made me think I was on the set of a Masterpiece Theatre production. I went to move the Ghia and get my L.L. Bean canvas duffel bag, which I had bought with the parka in a flush moment after an insurance fraud case. I can only afford stuff from Bean's when I clear a big case. Fortunately, their stuff lasts forever.

I took a minute to call Danny's office. Danny was still in at six o'clock at night, and that made me wonder, the way detectives always do, why he wasn't on his way home to his wife. Was there trouble at home, or something better at the office? He was probably just working late. He sounded irritated on the phone when I told him where I was. He told me that her bank had advanced me another thousand dollars, which didn't bother me at all. I told him my room number and gave him the number of the hotel so he could reach me.

"Andy, don't turn this into a late vacation." Danny was using the tone that I was sure he used on the girls when they were about to do something he didn't like.

"Danny, what are you talking about?" It wasn't like him to get pissy with me.

"Andy, she is a big client, and I would like to keep her. I

would rather turn up no results than waste her money. I don't want to piss her off."

"Danny, we agreed that this was the next logical step. What is the problem?"

"Nothing. This one could be my shot, you know? Hey, don't worry about it. It's just one of those days in the office. You go out and find something."

"Sure, that is the plan, man." With that, he said good night, and that was it.

I decided that a meal and a drink might do me some good. The hotel information guide told me that they had something called the Taproom. I looked over the menu, and other than Welsh rarebit, I was not overly impressed. I decided that I would take a quick walk around town and see what there was. I picked up my parka and headed for the door. I walked down the stairs and through the tastefully furnished lobby with its sitting room off to one side. I pulled the parka on and went out and down the granite steps to the sidewalk.

To my right was a dark street that headed uphill and toward the church. I turned away from it and started toward the island's cobblestone Main Street. I passed a store that sold gourmet cookware and accessories. Everyone knows that everything tastes better cooked in Le Creuset. I passed a bunch of stores selling all sorts of clothes that I was sure I didn't want or couldn't afford. The top of Main Street was dominated by the brick Pacific National Bank, which was founded by money from the whaling trade and was now filled with real-estate money.

To call the town picturesque was an understatement. The center of town had two drugstores and was filled with shops with names like Buttner's, the Emporium, and the Ship Chandlery. The town was dripping with antique charm and architecture that hadn't changed in two hundred years.

I walked past restaurants that had interesting names and signs in the windows that let me know they were closed for the season.

Cars moved slowly by, but they were rare. I was the only person walking through the quiet town. When I had been there with Leslie during the summer, the uneven brick sidewalks of Main Street were packed with strolling tourists until ten or eleven at night. Everything had been open and the place was humming with activity. Now I was walking through a windy ghost town. All that was missing were the tumbleweeds.

I began to notice the breeze, which had picked up as it got darker, and I had turned into it. I could smell rain. I kept walking, listening to the sounds of my feet on the pavement. If this was a thriller movie on the Movie Loft, I would hear footsteps and someone would be following me. That was only in the movies.

When I had been in Vietnam, men were following me. They were trying very hard to kill me. There had been no footsteps in the dark or suspenseful music. Just tension, wound so tight in my chest that I felt like a long, coiled spring.

Every part of recon work was dangerous. The most dangerous part of a very dangerous job was the insertion. We picked our landing zones with care; we studied the area for days prior, reading intelligence reports, looking at maps and photographs. The helicopters would put us down in areas that the NVA couldn't imagine we would be in. Then they would rise up and loiter, waiting for us to tell them it was all clear. If not, they would swoop in and snatch us from harm. The time leading up to takeoff, my stomach would tighten. Once the bird was in the air, I would be going through all the stuff that had to happen in the first minutes on the ground.

Then we were on the ground. We radioed that we were all clear, and the choppers left. Then the great hunt began in earnest. We were hunting the NVA and the Viet Cong, trying to gather intelligence and call in ordinance on them. Kill them. They were hunting us. They had special units of men who would track us. They would fire single shots in the air as a signal if they were close to you.

One time as we were moving away from them, trying to avoid contact, I realized they were intentionally herding us toward a specific location. We could hear the herders; then we could hear more and more men moving. They were bringing in large numbers of men. They were pushing us toward a rock face, looking to envelop us and trap us against the rock face. If we were pushed up against it, we would be crushed under the sheer weight of their numbers.

Off to our left, I could hear trucks moving. There was a road that the NVA were using to push supplies down the Ho Chi Minh Trail. Roads were dangerous because there were so many enemy soldiers on them. We avoided roads at all costs, and when we had to cross them, we did so very quickly and carefully. Moving on a road, even a deserted one, was suicidal. Now we were going to run down one to get away from our pursuers. We were leaping out of the frying pan and into the bonfire. We had no choice.

We paused long enough to call the Covey Rider circling in the plane above, and we declared a "Prairie Fire." Prairie Fire was the code for troops in trouble, an emergency, life or death. We moved to the road, and when I saw a khaki pith helmet in front of me, I hosed the man wearing it with the K gun. 9mm rounds slammed into him and then the man behind him and then I turned to the man next to him. We threw grenades onto the road and into passing trucks.

I listened to the sound of the grenade spoons as they

made their whip-o-whirl noise as they flew off. It was an oddly pleasant noise that did not convey accurately what was to follow it. A few seconds later, it felt like everything on the road was exploding. The heat from the exploding trucks singed us, and oily flames reached out toward us. The smoke was thick, and the air was filled with screaming. The NVA routinely handcuffed their drivers to the steering wheels of the trucks to prevent them from abandoning them during air strikes. It was a hell of a way to fight a war.

We stepped onto the road, literally running for our lives. We fired at anything that moved, reloading as we ran, throwing more grenades and running a race where second place meant death. The heat was so intense that for a few seconds it was as if there was no humidity in the jungle. Our pursuers were momentarily shocked. No sane man would run down an NVA supply road, much less a whole team. It was enough of a pause to save us.

Rounds started whipping and whizzing by us. Dirt kicked up at our feet, and branches were snapping off of trees. When the road took a hard left, we kept going into the jungle. We stopped only long enough to throw grenades up and down the trail. Each man moving with an economy of motion.

Everybody except the man with the radio dropped their rucksacks on the go. One of the Yards smiled at me as he carefully put a hand grenade under one with the pin out. A curious NVA would lift the rucksack and get blown up. The Yard knew that, hence his brown-toothed smile.

I stopped and put in place two Claymore mines to discourage anyone following us. Then we ran more. We picked up a trail. Then the two loud booms of the Claymores and the screams of the NVA and the sound of shrapnel whizzing through the bush. They were close, very close. We kept moving down the trail. We stopped by a giant boulder, we put our last Claymores in front of it, and we got behind it in a file. In a few seconds, there were more booms and more screams. We stepped out and fired off a magazine each at the enemy; then we turned and ran.

The enemy slowed down enough that we were able to make it to an emergency LZ. We lay down in a circle, feet touching inside of it, a wagon wheel. We could still hear them, moving out in the jungle somewhere. They were picking up speed again. We could hear their cadre yelling at them to move faster.

We were in no shape to run or fight anymore. We were down to our last two magazines, and there were no more fragmentation grenades. Just one white phosphorous to signal the bird with. Our Team Leader was wounded, and one of the Yards had taken a round in his stomach. We heard them coming. When they were close, we popped the Willy Pete and watched its thick white column reach up to let the pilot know we were there.

Then we were on the birds heading back to the launch sight. That was what it was like when someone was following you trying to kill you. It was a frantic dash for your life.

Chapter 14

Bㅡut I wasn't in Vietnam. I was walking down a perfectly normal, perfectly quiet street in New England. That was the problem with my war. It just showed up uninvited all the time.

On my right, I passed a couple of inns and came to a stop partway up the small hill under a sign that was swinging in the evening breeze. The sign had a picture of a white man in colonial garb with horns coming out of his head, holding in one upraised hand a shackled black woman and child, and in the other upraised palm, a bag of money. Over one shoulder was a sailboat and over the other, a town with a windmill, obviously an homage to the island's whaling and trading days. Underneath, it said, GOOD FOOD, GOOD DRINK, GOOD COMPANY.

I pulled open the dark, wide-plank door by its wrought-iron handle. I stepped inside into a low, dark, narrow hallway. On one side to my right there was a cigarette machine—my brand was out. Next to it was a long, low, built-in wooden bench. To the left was a doorway flanked by two walls; half of each was made up of leaded glass window panes. On the other side of the doorway was a room with a low ceiling, dark timbers, and rough-hewn tables and chairs, all stained the color of molasses.

A woman, a girl more accurately, in her twenties, with Ivory Soap skin and brown hair in a ponytail came up to me. She was wearing blue jeans and a black sweater. She had a nice smile. She asked if I was there to eat and didn't seem upset that it was just me. We walked into the main room, and she led me around the corner to a table by an actual fireplace near the service bar.

The heat from the fire was nice after being outside. The table was the same simple molasses-colored plank affair as the rest, but smaller. It had a candle in a holder that was riveted to the tabletop and had a glass globe on top of it. There were windows around the room, and I could see that we were actually about four or five feet below street level. Behind me were some booths and an open door that led to the kitchen. The music coming over the speakers was a mix of electric guitar Bob Dylan, The Band, the All-man Brothers, and the occasional Johnny Cash song.

I had slid out of my parka by the time she came back with a menu that was printed on a blue sheet of paper that was newspaper-sized. On one side, it had a printed history of the island, the building, and the restaurant, and on the other was the menu.

"What do you want to drink?"

"Löwenbräu?"

"Sure . . ." She turned away, then turned back. "You look like you were outside and could use something to warm you up. You should try a hot toddy. You can always get the Löwenbräu when you warm up."

"That is a great idea."

She smiled brightly. "Okay, let me get that while you look at the menu. I'll be back in a sec." She turned, and her ponytail flipped as if to punctuate her movement. The menu had the standard fish and chips and fried clams, as well as sandwiches and burgers. There was nothing on it that looked notable, except for the fact that they seemed to offer everything just a little bit differently than I had seen anywhere else.

She came back with my hot toddy and set it down in front of me.

"Here, this should warm you up." Her smile was bright; the dim light and flickering fire conspired to make her look like someone too pure and pretty to be in a Chandler novel. She brought me back to reality by taking my order for a cup of chowder and cheeseburger with Boursin cheese. I sipped the toddy, which was hot, and at first I could just taste the rum, but then I could taste butter and cinnamon, and there was a hint of citrus. It was a drink that started off with the small, mean taste of the rum, but then opened up big and loud with all the notes and flavors it had. The Ivory Soap girl of a waitress was right—it did warm me up.

I still had the Crumley novel in my pocket, so I took it out. I read by the dim light of the candle, enjoying the heat from the fire and the warmth from the toddy. I would look up to watch the occasional person walk into the room or go by outside. Outside, I could only see ankle and shoe and not much else. I felt somewhat the way I imagined Ishmael did in the beginning of *Moby Dick*, while he is on Nantucket waiting for a whaling ship to go to sea on. I was sure that it was cold and windy out, and I was lucky enough to be inside by the fire with a good book and warm drink.

"What are you reading?" She had brought back my chowder and set it down next to me with oyster crackers. There was a pat of butter melting in the chowder. I had expected her to say "watcha" and "chowdah," but her annunciation was clear and proper. I held out the book for her to see in the dim light.

"Never heard of him. What's it about?" Her brow had furrowed slightly, and combined with her Ivory Girl clean-cut good looks, it made my heart beat faster.

"It's a detective novel about a guy who is trying to find someone for a mysterious woman. The hero is a little different. It isn't great literature, but the writer has a real nice way with words." I was pretty sure that it wasn't her type of thing.

"Not what I normally read." She smiled brightly. "Maybe I'll check it out if I get sick of what I am reading now. Enjoy the chowder." She turned away and was gone.

I opened the packet of oyster crackers and poured it into the chowder. I ate it slowly while reading about how it is done in the world of written words. The chowder was good, thick and warm, the type that my father would have told me to eat because it would "stick to your ribs." Crumley's hero was also good. He was the sort of disheveled antihero who walked out of the post–World War II morality, tripped on Korea, and landed on his ass in the world after Vietnam. He was a student of Chandler's observations that the detective as a fictional character had to be a loner. The empty chowder cup and toddy glass were replaced by the hamburger and a Löwenbräu. The Ivory Soap girl asked if I needed anything else, and I assured her I didn't.

The burger was a large, hand-formed patty, shaped more like a grenade than the disc of gray meat that passes for a burger these days. It was topped with Boursin cheese that was already beginning to melt a little and run down the sides with the burger's juices. The bun was a large roll that I was sure came from a local bakery and not some supermarket. The French fries were actually curls of potato, and while I had traveled some, I hadn't ever seen fries that were anything other than the straight, crispy, salted pieces of potato that we had all become accustomed to. I took a large bite of the burger and knew that I had made the right choice. All the injuries and injustices inflicted upon me by the cruel world were made up for with one bite of that hamburger, Boursin cheese, and freshly baked bun.

I ate the hamburger and most of the potatoes, but in the end, I couldn't finish it all. I also had two beers and worked my way through most of the Crumley novel. When the Ivory Soap girl came by to ask if I wanted anything else, I asked for another hot toddy for dessert. She brought it with the check and a smile that lit up my dark corner booth like a flashbulb. I put a very modest amount of Mrs. Swift's money down on the table to include a generous tip. I finished the toddy and the novel.

I walked out of the dimly lit restaurant, stopping only long enough to put on my coat. I pushed open the heavy wooden door and stepped outside. The wind had died down, but the night was clear and cool. Looking up, I could see the many pinpricks of stars in the night sky. I put a Lucky in my mouth and lit it. I walked toward my hotel, past an interesting-looking bookshop that was closed for the night. I would have to come and check it out when it was open. I finished my cigarette in front of the hotel and crushed out the butt. I made my way upstairs to my room and called it a night.

The bed was comfortable, and I fell asleep fast on my full belly. When the dreams came, they were the usual ones about war and death and my personal powerlessness. Most of them were my mind rehashing and repackaging my time in Vietnam. Some of them had nothing to do with any of it. In one, I was in my old uniform and jungle kit. My web gear was old and broken in the way it gets patrol after patrol, day after tedious day. I was wearing all my old gear: knife, Browning Hi-Power pistol, grenades, D-rings, and I was carrying the silent Swedish K gun that I sometimes used. I was stalking—there is no polite way to say it—a person through the tall grass and reeds on the outskirts of Ruth Silvia's farm. I could hear people laughing, guitars playing, and I could smell a lot of weed smoke in the air. Up ahead, I spied a slim figure in black pajamas and a conical straw hat. I could see an AK-47, but I couldn't catch up to him. I picked up the pace and heard the laughter of Ruth Silvia's hippie followers in my ears. I finally got close and raised the K gun; I could feel the wire stock in my shoulder and the metal against my cheek. I looked through the sights, lining them up on the VC's back. Safety off, I squeezed the trigger all the way to the rear and heard only the *click*. It wasn't the felt-covered bolt silently moving back and forth, just the empty click of having made a fatal mistake. The VC turned, spilling the conical hat off of her head. It was the Ivory Soap girl waitress, her laughter mixed and mingled with Ruth Silvia's hippies. She raised the AK, and all I saw was her blinding smile.

I woke up with the sheets and blankets tangled around my legs. My head didn't hurt, but I can't say that it felt good, either. A bright ray of sun was stabbing through the room, and it hurt my eyes when it was on my face. I rolled over, but it was no use. I was awake. I lifted my watch off of the bedside table and saw that it was just after six. I had made a practice to never be up early after I left the army. I put the watch down and dragged myself out of bed for a hot shower.

I dressed more or less as I always did and headed downstairs in search of breakfast. The hotel offered some, but I decided instead to see if the diner I had seen the other night was open for breakfast. I walked down Centre Street, enjoying the cool morning air and smoking my first cigarette of the day. The sunshine that I had woken up to was gone. There was a light, chilly drizzle coming down, and I was beginning to see why the island was called the Gray Lady of the Sea.

Just off of Centre Street on India was a diner called The Dory, and it had a wooden sign swinging above the door telling me so. It was open early for breakfast, did lunch, but didn't bother with dinner. I walked in and was confronted by a narrow room. One wall to my right had a series of tables for four laid out down the length of the building. All of them were full. To my left was a counter and stools that ran most of the length of the building. On the other side of the counter was the flat-top grill, toasters, and a cash register. There was a TV on in the far corner, and the walls were brownish with pictures and clippings. I was able to get a seat on one of the stools at the counter, and a heavyset man with a five o'clock shadow put a menu down in front of me.

"Coffee?"

"Please." He went away and I looked at the menu, all of which looked to be what you would expect from a breakfast and lunch joint. He put coffee down in front of me in a brown ceramic mug.

"Cream? Sugar?"

"No, thanks."

"Know what you're having?"

I pointed to something on a plate going by that looked like a small, perfect pair of perky breasts.

"What is that?"

He smiled, showing me the end result of a lot of coffee and cigarettes.

"That is our world-famous eggs Benedict. Two sunny-side up eggs, on top of Canadian bacon, on top of an English muffin, topped with two olive halves, and covered with Hollandaise sauce."

"World famous?" I asked skeptically.

"World famous on Nantucket," he laughed. "Want 'em?"

"Sure, they look good. Thanks."

I picked up a discarded copy of the *Globe* that was laying on the counter. The headlines were all about cyanide in Tylenol. The economy was bad enough to make most people want to get a batch of the poisoned Tylenol. China had just reached a population of a billion people, and the president had told the Polish government just how annoyed he was with them. It was depressing stuff to read about. Reading about the Patriots wasn't any more cheerful. The weather was typical for fall in New England: cold, damp, and rainy.

The cook put the eggs Benedict down in front of me on an oval plate. He topped off my coffee without asking and moved down the line to attend to other customers. I ruined his artistic vision of perfect breasts by cutting into the eggs Benedict and taking a bite. I wondered if it would suffer for not being made with poached eggs, but it didn't. It didn't take me long to finish the coffee and eggs. I paid and walked out into the cool morning air.

It was still too early for the town offices to be open, so I decided to take a walk and have a smoke. I headed down India Street away from town. The street itself was made up of quaint houses, the newest of which was only about two hundred years old. At the end of India, I turned down Liberty Street and then on to North Liberty. Here the houses began to be a little less densely packed but still had plenty of charm. I followed North Liberty. On my right, there was a low-lying marsh, and to my left appeared to be just a large, open area of scrub pine and high grass.

I followed North Liberty past a small Cape Cod with a white picket fence and two Russian olive trees. I turned onto West Chester Street with its larger, newer homes, which slowly turned back into the older homes more in keeping with the island's history. On West Chester Street, the trees were taller and they were swinging. I walked along the uneven sidewalks until they brought me to Centre Street. I was at the bottom of the hill that was topped by one of the big white clapboard churches that can be seen from the ferry when it makes its way into the harbor.

The rain was picking up, and by the time I reached the brick two-story building that housed town hall and all of the town's offices, I was starting to squish when I took a step. I made my way inside and looked at the directory for a few seconds while the water dripped off of me and onto the floor. I followed the signs to the office that dealt with deeds and property. I found the appropriate frosted-glass door and made my way inside.

"My goodness, you look like a drowned rat." I could only see the top half of the woman behind the counter, but she looked to be a solid woman in her forties with dark hair and glasses that had oversized square lenses and bent metal frames. She was wearing a pale sweater to ward off the chill in the building.

"The rain picked up a little more than I thought it would." My hair was plastered against my head, and my beard was wet, which is never a good sign. I pushed lamely at my hair but knew it was a wasted effort. I unzipped the parka, which had done a good job of keeping me mostly dry.

"What can I do for you? I don't have any towels." She smiled, and I was pretty sure that someone somewhere on the island was a lucky man.

"I was hoping to see some deed maps and records." I smiled my most winning smile, which isn't saying much. "I promise not to drip on them."

"Of course, what are you looking for?" I told her the lot numbers I was interested in. They were the ones that included some of the larger undeveloped lots on the island and the piece that Ruth Silvia owned.

"Okay, give me a couple of minutes." She got up and walked toward the back of her office. She was tall, and the phrase "pioneer stock" made its way into my sodden head. I looked around the office, which had a series of black and white pictures of the island intermingled with the sort of informational posters that are in every municipal office in the world. I dripped and waited until she came back.

"Why are you interested in these? Are you a real-estate person?" Her brow was furrowed above the Tootsie glasses, and "real estate" was said the same way Father O'Malley used to say "fornicator."

"No, do I look like I have that type of money?" I tried my most charming smile again. "I'm working on my doctorate in local land use in New England towns. I'm focusing on how properties have changed over the years and the impact on the local community."

"Oh, I see. What school?" Her frown had eased up a little.

"B.U. Political Science."

"Aren't you a little old to be a student?"

"Blame the army. They insisted I take a break from my studies to help them out with a problem in Southeast Asia." Mentioning Vietnam, hinting at Vietnam was a great way to get most people to stop asking questions. No one wanted to talk about it.

"Okay, here they are. Let me know if you have any questions."

"Thanks." I spent fifteen minutes looking over maps that were of no interest to me, making meaningless notes in my slightly damp notebook. I also cross-referenced the deed maps with my tourist map of the island. Later, I would compare that to the street map that I had picked up in Boston before coming out to the island.

"Excuse me, miss?" I used my sincere voice. She looked up from her desk.

"Yes?" She leaned over, and I could smell a perfume of some sort but couldn't tell you what it was.

"I noticed that this one plot"—I pointed to a spot on the deed maps—"is one large plot, except for this one section at the edge of it. I noticed it is shaded differently?"

"That is a private plot that has been leased to the Cranberry Company. It is a very large cranberry bog."

"Cranberry Company?" I asked, genuinely curious.

"Yes, this is a large cranberry bog. It is responsible for the single largest crop that big company gets. If you drink cranberry juice or eat cranberry sauce on Thanksgiving, chances are some of it is from here." She smiled with civic pride.

"This section here is leased to the company?"

"Yes, has been for as long as I can remember."

"What do these black boxes here, here, and here mean?" I was pretty sure I knew the answer but wanted to hear her say it. Maps, all maps, have a lingua franca, part of which is that black boxes are buildings. The army had made me an expert at reading maps.

"Those are buildings used by the company to store machines and process the cranberries for shipment. That other one"—she stabbed a lacquered nail at the map—"that one is easy. It's the caretaker's house."

"Thank you."

She had pointed to the one black box in the middle of Ruth Silvia's plot of land. To me it looked just like the X on a treasure map from the old pirate movies.

I made my way out of the town offices and back out into the rain. I had spent a little over an hour in the municipal building. I didn't know if I had anything or not. I still had a plot of land that belonged to Ruth Silvia but was leased to the Cranberry Company. They had a caretaker who lived in that house, but that could be anyone. The only way to know would be to drive out there and see the caretaker.

I turned by the post office and walked down toward the water. I crossed over South Water Street and saw tucked away in a tiny building—more of a shed—was a tobacconist. I could smell the rich aroma of pipe tobacco. I could also smell wood smoke coming from the small chimney, and in the dampness of the rainy morning it was irresistible. I opened the door and stepped gratefully into the small, warm shop.

"Good morning. Let me know if I can be of help." He was a tall man with glasses, brown hair, and a beard to match. He had a small briar pipe sticking out of the corner of his mouth, filling the small shop with clouds of thick, pungent smoke. He was dressed in work boots, thick corduroys that were a faded brown, and had a green chamois shirt tucked into them. He favored suspenders and seemed so painfully thin that a belt would only make him seem thinner. He was sitting in a wooden captain's chair with his feet up against a woodstove, and a copy of *Wooden-Boat* magazine was open in his lap.

"Thanks. I was running low on cigarettes, but that pipe smoke smells so good I may have to take up the habit." I looked around and saw that he had racks of cigarettes;

many were brands that I had never even heard of. There was a small humidor stocked with cigars that took up half of one wall, and then there were shelves filled with clear jars of pipe tobacco. There was a cash register on the counter. In another corner, next to the stove, lay a yellow Lab sleeping the contented sleep of those dry and out of the rain.

"Well, let's get you set up with some cigarettes and see what we can do for a pipe." When he stood, he had to duck his head slightly. He walked over to one of the racks of cigarettes.

"What are you smoking now?" He said this over his shoulder to me.

"Lucky Strikes." I had been smoking Luckies since I had joined the army.

"I have those, but can I also recommend these?" He handed me a package of cigarettes with a picture of a bearded sailor inside a life ring that said, "Player's Navy Cut."

"Never heard of them." The box was flatter and wider than an American pack.

"They're English. They have a nice, rich flavor." He was a man who was clearly comfortable in his domain.

"Okay, I'll try a pack and see." He beamed around his pipe when I showed interest.

"You were also interested in a pipe and some tobacco?" He stooped forward a little.

"Yes, please. I have never smoked one before, but I think I am ready to try." His smile widened and still he managed to keep the pipe lodged in the corner of his mouth.

"I can suggest some pipes and show you how to pack and light them."

"That sounds like just the thing." He pulled some pipes of varying sizes and shapes from the wall. He explained the difference between bent and straight stems to me, as well as the difference between briars, meerschaums, and other types of pipe. I settled on a briar with a slight curve but not a deep bend in the stem. The bowl wasn't overly large, and the price was affordable. He seasoned the bowl with honey and explained that it would take about ten different smoking sessions before it would be truly seasoned, and to start by smoking half bowls.

"Do you have any ideas about what type of tobacco you would like?" He had the gravity and solicitousness of an undertaker.

"I would like something flavorful, rich, but none of those apple- or cherry-flavored tobaccos." I could never stand to be anywhere someone was smoking something that smelled like it came from inside a candy factory. He came out from around his counter and stood meditating in front of his glass jars. He eventually placed three on the counter and removed the lids. He explained the differences to me, and I ended up with two ounces of a rich Turkish blend, cut with a healthy dose of Cavendish. I ended up buying a tool to clean and scrape the bowl with, as well as a tamp for the burning tobacco, pipe cleaners, and two boxes of wooden matches.

"When I am not on island for the rainy season, I live in Boston. You wouldn't happen to know of a good tobacconist there, would you?"

"In Boston, there are a few, but there is really only one: L.J. Peretti's." He told me the address, which was by the Greyhound bus station near the Common and on the edge of the Combat Zone.

"Now you have everything you need to start smoking." He smiled as he watched me pack and light a bowl. His smile widened as the plumes of smoke further obscured the interior of his shop.

"Yup, I am a regular Inspector *Maigret* now." I figured he was one of the few people who might get the reference.

"*Oui*, monsieur," he said with his Cheshire cat's grin as he put my money away in his cash register.

I stepped out into the drizzle, feeling a little bit better about life in general. I walked down by the water, smoking my new pipe, wishing I had a fedora, but nonetheless enjoying the nostalgic scene. I walked down Easy Street by the water, trying to figure out my next move. I had to go to the caretaker's. He probably wasn't Charlie Hammond, and that meant that my investigation would be pretty much over.

I made my way back to the hotel, and by the time I got there my pipe had pretty much gone out. I went upstairs to change into some dry clothes and figure out lunch. Upstairs, I found dry jeans, a shirt, and socks but had to put on my wet shoes. They squished water out of them as I made my way back down the stairs. My parka was damp, and it seeped through my shirt in no time.

Outside, the wind had picked up and smacked me in the face hard enough to make my eyes water and to make me wonder why people lived on the island all year-round. The wind coupled with my damp clothes was enough to convince me not to be a hero but to duck into the Brotherhood, where I had dinner the night before.

The Ivory Soap girl walked over to me. She was wearing blue jeans and a black sweater that gave me a good idea about her curves. They were in all the right places, and I couldn't find fault with any of them. She was wearing heavy, square-toed, leather boots that clunked on the floor as she led me to a table by the fireplace.

"You look like you could use some drying out in front

of the fire." She smiled, and I was pretty sure she could have sold toothpaste for a living.

"Thanks, you mean I look like a drowned rat." I was pretty sure that my hair, which was too long, was a soggy mess.

"More like one of those stray tomcats that gets caught in the rain. The kind that has been living outside on its own for so long that he doesn't realize there is something to be said for living inside and having someone take care of him." Her smile curled a little bit at the corner of her mouth with the cruel playfulness that all women have. I was pretty sure that in this game of cat and mouse that, no matter what she said, I wasn't the cat.

"That sounds about right."

"Can I get you a drink? You look like you could use a hot toddy even more than you did last night."

"Please. It is nasty out there." She put a menu down in front of me and left to get my much-needed drink. I took off my coat and hung it over the chair by the fire. I sat and stared alternately at the fire and at the rain splashing outside the window. The waitress came back and put the steaming toddy down in front of me.

"Well, what are you having, Mr. Tomcat?" She smiled again and I felt like I was about ten years old. I ordered a cup of soup and half a sandwich from the menu. I watched her ponytail swish from side to side as she walked away.

I was not sure what the best way to go about the business of figuring out where Charlie Hammond was. There wasn't any way that I could see to finesse the situation. I could stake out the caretaker's cottage, but that could take days, and I was pretty sure that would draw a lot of attention. I was sure that Mrs. Swift's patience was not infinite. The only way I could see to do things was just to drive out there under some pretense and figure it out as I went along.

My soup and sandwich came with a smile and some gentle banter but not much else. It was good, and between that, the pretty waitress, and the toddy, I started to feel warm again. I was starting to see why people would live on the island year-round. When I was done, I slid some money down on the check, leaving a larger tip than I should have, but I am a sucker for a pretty smile and some witty conversation.

Chapter 15

I walked up the street and to the back of the hotel, where the Ghia was parked in the lot. I lit the pipe and sat slowly puffing on it as the mist cleared from the windshield and the wipers beat the rain away from it. I turned the radio on and eased out of the parking lot. I had to box my way around several blocks because of all of the one-way streets but eventually made my way to Orange Street. The Ghia slid up the hill, and I put a Steely Dan cassette into the tape player. Their mellowness went well with the pipe and the rain.

I followed Orange Street out of town past the densely packed houses that had been there for two centuries. I passed a package store, a bakery, a convenience store, a gas station that was also a package store, and just beyond that, a pizza joint and the Island Home for the Aged before I came to the rotary. I went around the rotary, past a bored-looking cop sitting in his cruiser in a parking lot, and turned onto Milestone Road. The houses and businesses fell away, and the road was bordered on both sides by scrub pines and telephone poles. Every mile or so there was a white-painted stone marker that gave the road its name. I followed the road out of town and up a hill, one of the few on the island, and at the top I could see the bogs below me and off to the north.

The wind was pushing the Ghia around like it was a toy, and between that and the rain it was taking a little effort to keep her on the road. I came down off of the hill, and the wind eased up a little bit, but the rain had picked up noticeably. Steely Dan was nice and mellow, and the inside of the Ghia was filled with pleasant-smelling pipe smoke.

I passed the road that I wanted to turn onto twice before I realized where it was. The Ghia bumped over the tarmac that was cracked from a few hard winters and a tight budget. The day was dark enough, but the road was darker still because of a wall of scrub pines, beach plums, and grapevines that were growing on either side of the narrow road. I slowed the Ghia down to a crawl, looking for the next road that I had to turn down. I didn't like the idea of having to turn around on the narrow road.

The road that I wanted was a dirt road. Dirt was misleading; like all of the roads in the area, it was actually white packed sand. The Ghia turned off of the tar and onto the sand with a bump. I shifted into a lower gear and nudged the old girl down the road. The rear end of the Ghia occasionally slewed a little in a patch of soft sand but would right itself. The road couldn't have been more than half a mile long but seemed to take a long time. I came around a corner and found myself in the driveway and front yard of a small house. I cut the wheel hard to the side and hit the brakes in order to stay in the driveway and not plow into the house or the shed. The Ghia and I bumped to a stop faced the way we had initially come in. I let out a small oath and shut off the car.

I stepped out into the rain and looked at what I had almost hit. The shed was small—bigger than a tool shed but much smaller than a barn. It turned out to be an old two-car garage, the kind with double wooden doors that open out and a series of small windows across the top, instead of the standard garage door that rolls up. The shed had one wall with fishing nets and lobster pot buoys hanging on it. There was a pile of lobster pots stacked up against the shed.

The house was a small Cape with the low roof facing north. It had smallish windows and a solid wooden front door. It was small and looked like a warm, good place to be on a cold, wet, early-November afternoon. Both the garage and the house were covered in cedar shingles that had weathered silver gray. The house had gray trim, and a redbrick chimney rose over the center of it. There was a light by the front door, but it was turned off.

There was a faint smell of wood smoke, but nothing was coming out of the chimney. It was quiet except for the sound of the Ghia's engine cooling and the rain bouncing off of the car. I went to the front door and knocked. I couldn't hear anything as I waited. I knocked again, and again nothing. The windows had curtains drawn, and I tried the door, but it was locked. I walked over to the garage, but the doors were locked, and I couldn't see anything through the window on the side.

Rain was making its way down my collar, and I was getting colder. I was also in a pickle. I could find my way inside the house or the garage, but that was risky. The caretaker could come home at any time and wonder why some armed stranger was in his house. Then the police might take interest, and I could find myself without a license. For a missing person case, that just didn't seem worth it. Also, I would end up tracking mud everywhere, which didn't strike me as the subtlest way of going about it. It was too soon to snoop, too soon to run amok.

Instead I went and sat in the Ghia. With engine on and the smell of my now-long-cold pipe, it was warm and pleasant. Steely Dan sang songs to me, and I wondered how long I would wait for the caretaker to come home. I smacked the ashes from the pipe into my palm and left them in the yard, where they washed away. In the end, it wasn't long.

I was damp, chilled, and uncomfortable. It was getting darker, and tomorrow was another day. I decided to head into town to see if I could find somewhere to buy dry shoes and maybe a sweater. I took the dirt road slower and then bumped over the uneven tar until I got back to Milestone Road. The Steely Dan tape had come to its end, and I turned on the radio to find Jim Morrison and The Doors screaming at me from one of their concerts. It was discordant and jangled at me and reminded me of Southeast Asia, the euphemism that we all now used for the dirty word . . . Vietnam.

I headed back into town feeling like I had just missed a pop fly in a Little League game. I wasn't sure why, but it just felt like I had blown an opportunity. As I passed the houses, I could catch glimpses of dark gray skies, salt marshes, and a bit of the harbor. I parked the Ghia in front of a store that looked like it would have what I wanted. I went inside and in record time bought work boots, a chamois shirt, a khaki shirt, and a fishermen's cable knit sweater. I paid twice what I would have on the mainland, but I was cold and wet. Next to the clothing store was a liquor store, where I bought the world's most expensive bottle of Cutty Sark scotch. I also stopped at the hardware store around the corner and bought a bottle of sewing machine oil and a couple of bandanas.

I made my way back to the hotel and parked in the lot behind it. There were no messages at the desk and nothing new. I went upstairs with my already sodden paper bags and let myself into the room. I hung my jacket over the back of a chair near the radiator in some vain hope that it would dry out. From there I went into a hot shower.

When I came out, I could hear the rain beating against my window. I poured myself a belt of the Cutty Sark and took a sip. The fire made its way down to the center of me, and I was starting to feel warm. I took the Colt out of its holster and slid the magazine out of the heel of the pistol, then flicked off the safety and racked the round out of the chamber. I slid the rounds out of the magazine and sat them upright on the desktop. I did the same with the spare magazine. I took the pistol apart and wiped as much of the moisture off of it as I could with one of the bandanas. I put some oil on the other bandana and wiped it onto the pistol.

It was methodical work that I had done thousands of times in my life. After a while it becomes muscle memory, and you don't think about what you are doing. It was the same with a missing person case ... maybe I had just been going through the motions but not really thinking about them. Once I was satisfied the gun was well oiled, I put it together again. I wiped out the magazines, oiled and reloaded them. When it was all done, I put one in the pistol and chambered a round. Maybe I needed to take another look at this case. I slid the magazine out and topped it off.

It felt comforting to clean the pistol. It was repetitive, and I was able to clear my head. Now I found that something was nagging me. I was beginning to wonder if I had missed something. I pulled out the case file and the yellow legal pad with my scribbled notes and started to skim through them. I pulled out a fresh legal pad to make notes on. I was curious about the neighborhoods that Charlie Hammond had lived in, or at least where the checks went.

I came up with a list of questions related to the time that he was in each city. They amounted to: What was the neighborhood like? What type of people lived there? Were there any case reports from the specific addresses, with the exceptions of the mailboxes? Was there anything that stood out in particular?

I picked up the phone and was lucky to get Danny on the first try.

"Tell me you found the guy?" he asked halfheartedly.

"Nope, not yet." I caught myself shrugging as I said it.

"Please tell me you don't need more money. I am getting calls daily from Swift's people asking me for progress reports." He sounded a little harried.

"No, the money is fine. Actually, I was hoping that your assistant could make a few calls for me and ask some questions." It was actually worse than asking him for money.

"I thought you were the investigator who gets paid to investigate?" He definitely sounded pissed off.

"I am, and I do. I have some legwork that I need done, and for me to do it will take time and money that you don't seem to think I have. On the other hand, you have an assistant and a couple of underpaid paralegals . . ." I trailed off, hoping he would get the drift.

"Okay, who do you need called?" He didn't like giving in, even for something small like this. Danny hated to lose any contest. It had been like that when we were little kids. Losing a marble or two would have him in a funk for the rest of the day. He got to be such a pain in the ass I would let him win them back every time we played.

"I need you to contact the police departments in LA, Las Vegas, Seattle, and San Francisco. I need you to call around and ask some questions about the addresses that Hammond lived at when he lived there. I need to know what was going on there at the time, and if there was any police activity during the times that he was at those addresses. Tell your people not to talk to a desk clerk but someone from Detectives or Narcotics." I then read him the list of questions I had come up with.

"Okay, I will see what we can come up with. I have some interns that I can use. It might take a couple of days. What are you looking for?" He was less on edge now that he was assured that I was actually working on something and not just vacationing with his client's money. The client that he was making out to be his ticket to being mistaken for a respectable WASP.

"I am not sure, but I will know it when I see it."

"What are you going to do now?"

"Now? Now I am going to go get some dinner."

Danny said some bad words that I am too polite to repeat and slammed the phone down. I washed my hands to get rid of any trace of sewing machine oil. I finished my whiskey and took my own advice about dinner.

My new work boots were stiff, and the fishermen's sweater itched where it rubbed against my chin. The khaki shirt saved most of my neck from the itchy sweater. My jacket from Bean's was damp, but with the sweater on it didn't matter too much. I had slid the .32 in between my belt and jeans, where it was held pretty snugly in place and couldn't be seen under the sweater.

The rain had settled into a chilly drizzle and mist. I walked past the Brotherhood, having eaten there twice in less than two days. The wind was still blowing, but the sweater was warm and my feet were dry, so I didn't mind being on foot. Off in the distance I could hear the foghorn blowing its mournful two-note song. This was Sam Spade weather, but this wasn't San Francisco.

I took care crossing the street in the fog. I was headed downhill toward the water. In my walks around town I had seen the Atlantic Café, which looked like it had a nice, warm bar for a cold night. The Atlantic Café wasn't far from the Greek Revival Athenaeum building and its nice garden. It wasn't an unpleasant walk in the fog and chill. It reminded me of a Sherlock Holmes story. Somewhere there should have been a hound howling.

I pulled open the door and stepped out of the raw damp into a warm, smoke-filled bar that was half full of regulars. The lights were soft, but not dim. There were people sitting at tables, having dinner, and I opted for a high stool at the bar. The music didn't stop, and none of the locals looked at me as though I didn't belong, so that was a start.

I found a seat at the bar, and the bartender slid over. He was tall and had one of those tans that spoke of a life of sailing and surfing, and skiing in the winter. He brought me a Löwenbräu and a menu when I asked for them. On the TV, they were showing a football game that I wasn't that interested in, but at regular intervals people cheered or booed. The bartender came back and took my order for a cup of French onion soup and prime rib with a baked potato. He seemed more interested in the game on TV than making small talk with me. I wasn't complaining. I was thinking about the little cottage by the bogs and how I hadn't found out anything about the owner. I hadn't come any closer to finding the elusive Charlie Hammond or even finding out if he was still alive.

I had finished my food, and the game was winding down. I looked out at the fog and decided that I was in no rush to go out in it. I was uncertain about what the next move was. I had to come up with something or Danny would be pissed, and he would have to tell Deborah Swift to pull the plug on the investigation, or at least my being a part of it. I was going over it all in my head, trying to find some little thread that I had missed, when I felt a hand on my elbow and heard a gentle, mocking voice in my ear.

Chapter 16

"Tomcat, you finally found your way out of the rain?" I turned and saw the waitress from the Brotherhood at my elbow. She was smiling, and her eyes glinted in the bar's dim light. She was wearing faded blue jeans and a dark turtleneck sweater. Saying she looked good was like saying the John Hancock building had a couple of windows.

"Even tomcats get sick of being wet. What about you? Will the people at the Brotherhood be upset with you for being in another bar?"

She laughed, and it was a nice sound. "No, on an island this small no one holds it against you when you go out." She slid onto the seat next to me without asking or being invited. I was not one to protest. The bartender slid over the way they do when a woman sits down at the bar.

"Hiya, Shelly, what'll it be?" he said, directing all the warmth at her that he was unwilling to squander on the likes of me.

"Hiya, Rolling Rock and another for him." She jerked her left thumb in my direction.

"What brings you out to the island, Tomcat? You don't seem the tourist type . . . too serious by far?" Her smile was a little crooked in one corner, and her nose was button cute and wrinkled slightly when she smiled. She had the type of All-American good looks that sold a lot of soap and shampoo.

"Andy, not Tomcat. Would you believe me if I told you that I was on sabbatical?" I attempted a smile and was pretty sure that she thought I was in the middle of a muscle spasm. She shook her head slowly with mock seriousness and slightly pouty lips.

"Maybe I am out here looking for someone?" I tried not to sound too serious.

"Tomcat," she said, clearly ignoring my perfectly good, perfectly nice, normal name, "that is so sweet that you came out here and have been looking for a girl like me." Her sarcasm was honey-coated but sarcasm all the same.

"I won't deny that you are what I have been looking for, but you are not the who I am looking for." I wasn't good at flirting or witty repartee, but I was making up for that with effort.

"Next you are going to ask me what a girl like me is doing in a place like this." She smiled again, and I saw incisors and started to wonder again if I was not the cat in the game of cat and mouse.

"I hope I wouldn't be so clichéd if I asked you that. Maybe I might say something along the lines of 'What brought you out here to the island?'"

"Not bad. What makes you think that I am not a native daughter of the Gray Lady of the Sea?" She leaned back against her chair.

"Your accent is wrong. A little Midwest, a little flat . . . maybe a hint of the South, a lot of things, but you are not from around here." I tried smiling again, and my face must have loosened up because it seemed easier.

"You aren't wrong. I moved around a lot. My dad was in the air force."

"Aha . . . but that doesn't tell me anything about why you are out here."

"Art."

"Art? Who is Art?"

"Not a him, but an it. I am a graduate student at Brown. I came out to work in a gallery and on my thesis . . . eleven months later, I am still here and my thesis is stalled."

"What is your thesis about?" I was pretty sure that I was not interested, but it seemed wrong not to ask.

"I am not sure anymore. I started off writing about the effects of the Great Depression on twentieth-century art. Now it has kind of evolved into the study of a couple specific artists and the effects of the Depression on their art." She paused to drink from the green glass bottle that the bartender had placed in front of her. "Or maybe the effects of the Depression on the works of a couple of artists."

"Out here? This doesn't strike me a big artist's community." I drank from my own green bottle.

"You'd be surprised. A lot of artists came out here in the thirties and forties. It was close to New York; they could rent little beach shacks for studios. The island wasn't crowded in the summertime like it is now. If someone wanted some peace and quiet and a place to write or paint, this was it."

"And that is what brought you out here?" I was one hell of a detective.

"There are a couple of those artists who still live out here, and the gallery that I work at features a lot of their work from the postwar period. It is a pretty unique opportunity to see their original works and interview them." She was looking at me directly with large, unblinking blue eyes.

"It sounds like you are in the right place to work on your thesis." I took another pull on my bottle of beer and didn't ask the obvious question about why her thesis was stalled.

"You are wondering why if I am in this great place, with access to these great paintings and the artists themselves, my thesis is stalled?" Her gaze was more direct as though challenging me.

"I was curious, but it isn't for me to pry. I would imagine that writing a thesis paper isn't easy." I had known a lot of people who hadn't been able to finish them. I hadn't been able to start one.

"Have you ever been hungry? Not the type of hunger from being a few hours late for a meal, but that real, deep hunger that makes you shaky?" She was looking at me with an intense expression, brows knitted, and eyes searching my face for any trace of mocking.

"Yeah, I've been that hungry." I was always hungry in Basic Training, we all were. It was all the PT, all the marching, and all the learning how to kill. The army wanted its killers to be lean and hungry. Later, Airborne school; more running, more PT, then running around the woods trying to earn my Green Beret, and then, much later, in the steamy jungle after having to ditch my pack and run for an extraction point. I had been hungry and lean. I had been young, and it was two lifetimes ago, but I still remember being hungry and scared.

"Well, when you were hungry and you could suddenly eat—eat anything you wanted—was it tough to decide what to have?" She hadn't stopped looking me in the face with the same intense expression.

"Yeah, I know what you are saying." It hadn't been

hard to decide, but I understood what she was reaching for. She was picking at the white writing on the bottle that wouldn't come off. Her fingernail was making a slight popping noise against the raised lettering. The bartender brought us another round without our asking, and we didn't complain about it. We didn't complain when another round showed up after that one, or a couple of thick, short shot glasses with amber bourbon to warm us from the chill of night.

"Well, Tomcat, what really brings you out here? You aren't looking for someone; no, you are running away, like most people who end up here." She sipped off of the top of the bourbon shot and shuddered a little.

"Maybe they are the same thing. Maybe I am on some Zen journey to get lost and find myself." I smiled through my beard at her, but I can't say for sure that I wasn't leering at her.

"Tomcat, that is one of the funniest things I have heard in a long time. You are one of those shaggy tomcats, out in some back alley. A little unkempt." She tugged at my beard and tussled my shaggy hair. "Hungry and unkempt, like one of those cats that needs a good home, a saucer of milk, and is too stubborn to want to be anywhere but out in the alley on some rainy, cold night." She let go of my beard and went for another sip of the bourbon. I did, too, and felt it shudder and burn its way down to my stomach.

"Are you implying that all I need is the love of a good woman to fix what ails me?" I smiled as I thought about it. I had thought that Leslie had been the answer, but that hadn't worked out too well. I had been restless as long as I could remember, and it hadn't gotten better when I had come home from Vietnam. College wasn't the answer; I always sat near the window and looked out while the professor droned on. The cops hadn't been the answer; I knew it could have easily been me at the wrong end of the night-stick if things had been different.

"I don't know if you would take it if offered for more than a little while. You don't strike me as the type who is into permanence." She winked at me, and I wasn't sure she was wrong. I finished my bourbon and so did she, and the bartender refilled them.

"What makes you say that?" Now I was looking at her with a little bit of faux suspicion.

"It is the way you walked into the restaurant, or the way you were sitting at this bar. You don't mind being alone. Most people hate eating alone. You look like you prefer it. You sit quietly but never seem to be still. Those aren't the hallmarks of permanence."

"I hadn't ever thought of it that way. Let's just say that I prefer no company to bad company." More bourbon followed by cold beer.

"Tomcat, you are a mess. Maybe you don't know it, but you are. You may look like the actor from the remake of *King Kong* with your beard and shaggy sandy hair. You may smile, all charm through that beard, and your eyes might crinkle at the corners under that shaggy hair, and I am sure that you do all right for yourself most nights . . . but you are a mess." She drank down her bourbon and eyed me over the rim of the glass. She wasn't right about all of it, but she was right about enough of it.

She was sitting back against her chair and looking at me with eyes that were a little glassy and a smile that was a little loopy.

"Tomcat, they are getting ready to close for the night."

"That prospect makes me more than a little sad." It did make me sad. There are few things better than being out in a warm bar with a pretty girl on a damp, chilly night.

"Tomcat, we should go." With that, she stood up and

headed to the door. I was quick to follow after dropping cash on the bar. She stopped at the coat hook by the door and pulled on a yellow rain slicker. I put on my jacket, which wasn't damp anymore. Outside, under the lighted sign, she looked up at me and said, "Walk a girl home in this fog?"

"Of course, it would be the only chivalrous thing to do."

"So, you are some sort of gentleman?" She said it the same way she said Tomcat, poking fun at me.

"Something like that." It was foggy out and walking beside me, her head just came up a little bit over my shoulder.

"We'll see about that." She giggled, and off in the distance the foghorn replied. We walked down to the end of the block and turned toward the water. We ended up standing by a staircase leading up to the second floor of a wooden building that was perched over the water. The building faced the harbor, and on the other side, the ferry bobbed on its moorings.

"Tomcat, would you be offended if I asked you to come up and look at my etchings?" I could see her smiling up at me.

"I would be offended if you didn't."

I wasn't sure she could see me smile in the dark and the fog. She stepped close to me and held her face up to be kissed. I kissed her, slowly at first and then with more intensity. She smelled of tobacco, beer, and honeysuckle. She broke away and smiled up at me and said, "Emmn nice." She took my hand and led me up the stairs to her apartment. Her hand was small and warm against my own. The uncomfortable hunk of metal in my belt dug into my side, reminding me of its awkward presence. She unlocked the door, and we went into a small apartment, the closest thing the island had to a loft. Inside, the main room was dominated by what, after a few minutes, I realized was a fireplace, but appeared to be a large, upside-down, orange metal funnel raised three feet over an orange metal circle. The wall opposite the kitchen was made up of all windows and looked out on the water. Every wall that didn't have bookshelves in it had art prints push-pinned into it. They were nicely spaced and composed the way they would be if put there by someone who worked in a gallery.

"Tomcat, sit down. Make yourself comfortable. There is beer in the fridge and whiskey in the cabinet. I am going to slip into something more comfortable." She giggled at the end, but it didn't sound forced or clichéd. I skinned off the coat and slipped the Colt out and put it in the inside pocket. I folded my coat and put it on the floor next to the couch.

She came out a few minutes later wearing a T-shirt for a band that I had never heard of and a pair of panties that were cut high up on her thigh. Her hair was loose, and her breasts swelled against the T-shirt. She walked across the room toward me, all curves and moves like rolling seas. She got close to me, stood on tiptoes, put both arms around my neck, and pulled me down to her for a long, slow, wet kiss. It seemed to last for a long time and reminded me of necking at high school parties, the innocence and excitement and the need to literally come up for air.

She took a half step back and reached down at my sides for the sweater and pulled it up over my shirt. The sweater ended up on the floor near the couch. She slowly unbuttoned my shirt, and we kissed again. This time my hands found her, one on her young, large, and proud breast and the other on her beautiful bottom. She groaned, and her tongue worked against mine. Her hands were unbuttoning my shirt and finding their way in and onto my chest. I raised her T-shirt up, over her head, and while her arms were raised, I lowered my hungry mouth to her waiting, eager, hard nipples. She undid my belt and zipper; then her small, chilly hand was wrapped around me. We were both hungry and acted like it. She pushed me down on the couch and kneeled in front of me. Later I was kneeling in front of her, smelling only that most precious scent of hers. Eventually we were both naked on the couch. She ended up on my lap, facing me, with her legs wrapped around me and my hands under her beautiful and perfect bottom. When we were both spent, we laid on her couch.

She shivered, and I pulled her close. Her hands were running over my body.

"You're cold." I was the master of the obvious.

"Not so much." She snuggled into the hollow of my arm with her legs across my lap. Her scent was in my nose and on my lips.

"Do you want a blanket?" I was a gentleman of sorts.

"No, I want a fire." She showed me where I could find the kindling and wood, and in a few short minutes the room was filled with orange flickering light. We made love on the couch again, slowly, savoring each other. Later, she lit a joint and ran her hand over the scars on my chest, thighs, and back.

"Tomcat, you have been in a few fights." Assured statements from her sleepy mouth as her hands kept wandering over me. Little cartographers with dirty minds, but not without their fair share of sweetness, probing my most intimate secrets and nightmares that were recorded on my pale Boston Irish flesh.

"What else would you expect from an alley cat?" I said it with an uncomfortable smile.

"How? And don't tell me that you were in a car accident." She said it while two of her fingers were pushing on the entrance wound from where I was shot by an NVA with an AK-47. Her hand worked around to an ugly mass of scar tissue that was the exit wound.

"What would you believe?" Life had taught me that the truth was usually a negotiation.

"I know a bullet wound when I see one. My dad was stationed at Pope Air Force base. Fort Bragg was next door and a lot of GIs found their way to the pool. I've seen a few guys with bullet holes in them." Her voice was serious and her face set and stern and unbearably cute.

"That one, where your fingers are, is from an AK-47 round. I was running down a trail and the other guy was fast. I got hit." I had come around a bend, and there he was. He got off one round that hit me, but in his panic, had missed me after that. I had stitched him from crotch to head with the Swedish K gun. Its tubercular coughing was the sound of silenced death. I was lucky that he had missed the major artery in the shoulder and most of the bones. He was unlucky. Her hands worked around to my back, probing, feeling small scars.

"Shell fragments, from their mortars and our artillery, or maybe our mortars and their artillery." I shuddered involuntarily. It had been ugly, and when I have nightmares, it is about that incident. The sounds and smells and the fact that friends of mine died, those weren't memories that died easily. She rubbed a star-shaped wound on my butt.

"White phosphorous, a small piece from a grenade hit me in the ass." It was a crude wound. One of my Yards had been hit, and the grenade fell short, and I was too close. Later, one of my teammates dug out the burning WP with the tip of the ridiculous Fairbairn-Sykes knife he carried. It was a silly weapon for the jungle, but he had picked it up in Hong Kong on R&R, and there was no convincing him not to carry it. I was too quiet for too long when she grabbed my hair in two hands and kissed me hard on the mouth. Then she pulled my face by the beard down to her, kissing me hard, trying to make me forget it all, but her.

Later, lying in an itchy wool blanket in front of the dying embers of the fire in each other's arms, she ran her little hands through my beard and hair. We were close and warm, and I remembered what I was missing that most people had. Her voice, small and questioning, came through the dark to me.

"Vietnam?" In the dark, I could almost see how big her eyes were.

"Yes." That was the understatement of the century. The launch sites, the patrols, the cross-border missions were a different war in the same country. At first, I was scared and sure I would be killed or maimed. Then I stopped caring if I would be killed and only gave a shit about going out on missions. Once I stopped caring, it was easier. Then I just cared about going outside of the wire.

"What did you do?" She was young and sincere, and Americans were just coming to grips with how they had shit on us when we came home. On the other hand, every POL specialist, supply clerk, jerk, and bottle washer claimed they were Special Forces now.

"Nothing that makes sense anymore." That was the last time my life made sense. Everything had been logical, even the absurd and obscene. There was clarity to it all. It was simple. You did your job, you lived or you died, but there wasn't much confusion. Sometimes people died because they were unlucky or because they made a mistake or because the NVA got lucky.

I was a Green Beret. Just like the song. I went out and found the enemy and killed them or helped them get killed by our artillery and/or Air Force. We trained hard, small, nut-brown Montagnards to kill them with our leadership. We tried to kill the NVA, and they tried to kill us. We were all part of some elaborate chess game around the Ho Chi Minh Trail.

We were a small, tight-knit group who almost didn't exist anymore. We were an endangered species, an anomaly not welcome in our country or in society. I didn't have many friends left alive, and the ones who were I didn't hear from all that often. The occasional rambling, incomprehensible letter in spidery handwriting, or late-night drunken phone call made up all the communication we had anymore. We all had the same open wound that we could share, but we couldn't talk about it.

Somewhere in all of the soft whispering that new lovers do, we fell asleep on the couch. I woke up uncomfortable and cold. She was lying on her side with the blanket, and I was vainly clinging to a couple of inches of the couch. I slid or fell off of it. I stood and picked her up. I carried her to her bed and put her in it. I was shivering by the time I crawled in next to her. She was warm, and I did my best imitation of a barnacle next to her. She turned toward me and held me close.

"This is nice," she said, then began to snore softly. I fell asleep again and didn't dream about much of anything, which was all right with me. When I woke up, it wasn't dark, and the light outside of her windows was gray. My arm was stiff from where she had been sleeping on it. I lay in the bed listening to her breathing softly for a while. I knew that I wasn't going to fall asleep again. I managed to slip out of the bed without waking her up.

I found my clothes in the living room. I dressed quickly, shivering in the cold apartment. When I was dressed, I slipped the pistol back in my belt and pulled the sweater over it. I went into the kitchen, found a pen, and started quietly rummaging through drawers to find some paper.

"Slinking away, Tom?" She was standing in the bedroom door with the wool blanket wrapped around her. Her hair was wild, but her eyes were twinkling, and she smiled at me.

"Actually, I was looking for a piece of paper, so I could leave you a note." I smiled back.

"What would the note say? Thanks, I'll call you?" She was still smiling, and I was pretty sure that we were back to the game of cat and mouse and again, I still wasn't the cat.

"It was going to say that last night was nice. I was going to leave you the number where I am staying and tell you that I'd like to see you again." I felt like I was testifying in court.

"See me again . . . like a date or something?"

"Exactly like a date or something." She was smiling, and I wasn't sure I wasn't saying the wrong things.

"Well, Tom, I will say this—you are a little old-fashioned, but you are sweet." She walked over to me and put her arms around my neck and kissed me again. "I am off tonight. Why don't you swing by around seven, and we can get some dinner?" It wasn't a question.

"Okay. Seven it is." I told her where I was staying, and she nodded. I put my coat on and headed to the door. She kissed me again and locked the door behind me. I went down the steps and began to walk back to my hotel through the early-morning mist. Once in a while the fog would be pierced by slow-moving headlights. The foghorn kept booming off in the distance.

I felt good, and I could smell her on my hands and in my beard. I unconsciously would lift my hand to my face if only to reassure myself that last night had been real. That I had made love to her and that I wasn't dreaming. I was going back to the hotel to shower and eat but found that my feet took me to The Dory instead. Inside, everyone and everything was the same. There was a spot at the counter for me, a brown porcelain mug of coffee, and the same cook.

I ordered the eggs Benedict again. After the last night, how could I turn down breast-shaped food? I drank my coffee and picked up a copy of the *Globe* that was sitting on the counter. There was more in it about the blowup at the trade talks with the Japanese. The president was still angry at the Communists in Poland, but he was pretty much angry with all the Communists everywhere. Three Irish cops got blown up in Ireland, leaving a huge hole and more killings to come. I ate my breakfast and read the depressing news, paid my bill, and walked back to the hotel.

Chapter 17

Inside, there was only a message to call Danny, which I ignored, because I was pretty sure that he would accuse me of using Deborah Swift's money to get laid. I got in the shower, running it hot enough to sting, and then after I had washed off, turned it to cold and shivered for a few seconds of penance. I dressed in my usual faded jeans, new boots, white shirt, and corduroy jacket. The Colt .32 was back in the shoulder holster, under my left arm.

The Ghia was where I left her and she started with only a mild protest. The radio stations on the Cape weren't playing anything that I wanted to listen to, so I put in one of the tapes from The Band's ever-excellent *The Last Waltz* concert. I steered the Ghia through the town and out to Milestone Road. The fog had burned off, and a brittle fall sun shone on the Ghia's windscreen when I turned off onto the sand path leading to the caretaker's cottage. This time I pulled in without almost hitting any buildings or other standing objects.

I was rewarded by seeing what had once been a GMC pickup truck. It had started its life as a metallic green pickup truck with a big Detroit engine and a thirst for gas like no other. Now, only the cab was metallic green. The bed was gone, replaced by a series of wooden 4×4s that made up a flat platform. Resting on the platform, up against the back of the cab, was a red plastic twenty-gallon gas tank. It was the kind that is usually reserved for outboard engines, but in this case, a black rubberized hose ran from the tank and disappeared somewhere under the bed, inside the engine. It had Mass. plates on the back, and I wrote the number down out of habit. I parked behind it and got out of the Ghia. I unconsciously hitched my shoulders to readjust the pistol in its holster under my left arm.

I started toward the front door and was about to knock on it.

"Morning, friend. You need something?" I turned and there was a man standing a few feet behind me with a double-barrel shotgun pointed casually at the space between us. It seemed like everyone I was meeting these days had one. He was tall, with dark corduroy pants tucked into Wellingtons, an old, baggy gray sweater, and a purple chamois shirt over it. He had a craggy face that hadn't seen a razor in a few days. He had a salt and pepper ponytail topped by a leather tam-o'-shanter hat that was faded a soft caramel color. Nearby there was a volley of gunshots, two or three at the most, and I flinched. Actually, it was all I could do not to throw myself on the ground and crawl for cover. The war was never far away.

"Easy, fella, it is just a couple of the boys trying to get some birds out on the bog." He then said by way of clarification, "It is duck season." I nodded slowly.

"What brings you out here to the bog? You know this is private property?" His face was tan and had all the small lines and wrinkles that hard living will give you. This was that moment: to lie, not to lie, which half-truth to use?

"My name is Roark. I work for a lawyer concerned with a probate matter." It was, at the essence of it, true.

"Probate matter?" His eyes didn't seem to be entirely focused on me.

"Yes, probate, um . . . an inheritance." He looked at me for a minute.

"Inheritance. For me? Far out, man. I didn't even know, like, anyone had died." He smiled a goofy little smile, and I could see that he was missing a tooth on one side. I smiled, too, to let him know what a decent guy I was.

"Well, I didn't say it is your inheritance exactly. It deals with the will of an eccentric old lady with a few distant relatives."

"Distant relatives?" He was still smiling his goofy smile, and my face was starting to hurt from my own. He was still casually pointing the shotgun at the middle ground between us.

"Yes, a little old lady in Colorado died while owning most of a silver mine. She didn't have any heirs but should have a couple of distant relatives out there. Your name came up."

"Me, Ed Harriet? That is far out, man." His eyes were small, and I felt like he was looking at me calculating the range; then his eyes were just eyes again.

"Mr. Harriet, it isn't certain yet. I will have to talk to you and figure out if you are indeed related to the client. I just don't want to get your hopes up. It isn't certain that you are an heir."

"Are you a lawyer?" His smile was gone.

"No, I am just a guy hired by a lawyer to do some leg-work. I didn't even finish college."

"Oh, so, like, you want to talk to me, man?" He was smiling again, making me wonder how much pot this guy smoked.

"Yes, if you have the time."

"Sure, man, sure. Come on in, and we'll make some coffee." He led me around to the side of the house and a door that opened into a small kitchen. It was low and snug, with an actual fireplace in one corner and a stove in another. An avocado-colored refrigerator hummed against another wall. Across from the fireplace, under the window, was a sink. Near the fireplace, up against some windows, was a table covered with an old-looking oilcloth, with a few chairs up against it.

"Have a seat, man." He pointed a gnarled finger at one of the chairs by the table. I sat down on one and looked around the room, which had dark wood cabinets and prints of seascapes. Harriet leaned the shotgun in a corner. He then set about rummaging in cabinets and making coffee. He made it in a stovetop percolator, which stood out in my mind for some reason, but I couldn't tell you why it did. Maybe in a world filled with electric drip machines, a percolator seemed incongruous, or maybe it reminded me of a Philip Marlowe novel. Marlowe is always percolating his coffee. Harriet wasn't done there. He knelt in front of the hearth and unearthed some embers. When the fire was going, he stood up and smiled his loopy smile at me.

"That should take some of the chill off. How do you take your coffee? Cream? Sugar?"

"No, black. Thank you." He poured it into a chipped mug for me and made himself one with cream and sugar in a similar mug.

"So, were you, like, in the war? You know, Vietnam?" He spoke slowly as though he was concentrating on every syllable of every word.

"What gave me away? The flinching at the gunfire?"

"Yeah, man. I lived on a commune in Seattle one time. We had a few guys back from Nam. Guys who just wanted to get high and get laid and forget it. They had that same look in their eyes. Just like you."

"I am better now, but sometimes it sneaks up on me." Like when someone is standing in front of me with a shotgun and I hear gunfire.

"Yeah, I guess it never really leaves you. Where were you?" His eyes were big, and his voice was all California surfer.

"I was up north, but one shithole is as good as another in that country." I was at a place called Mai Loc and operated from there in places that Americans weren't supposed to be in. I was still in the habit of keeping my country's secrets by answering questions with vagaries, verbal sleights of hand, and half-truths. I was keeping secrets for people who let me down and I couldn't stand, about a war that no one wanted to talk about. My part was the one that no one wanted to admit had even happened. These days, talking about Vietnam was like talking about that relative serving hard time in a penitentiary. The stupid part of it was that I told them I would keep their secrets and still felt that my word had to mean something, even if theirs didn't.

"Yeah, yeah, was it bad, man?" His dark eyes were locked on my face, and I was not unsure that there was something a little hostile behind them.

"Yeah, it was bad." All I could think of was the artillery barrage. I could still hear it—the whistling, the explosions, and the screaming. I could still feel the air being knocked out of my lungs and being tossed around like a rag doll. I could still feel the pieces of hot metal ripping into me. I could taste the dirt, the dust, the shit, and the blood. I could still see the broken bodies of my friends and my enemies alike. I will forever wonder why I lived and they didn't. It was bad and it never left me. It never does, and I am not sure it is supposed to.

"Mr. Harriet, we should discuss the matter of the, um, potential inheritance. While it is not a large fortune, it is large enough to be worth some consideration."

"Well, man, I am not into material things, but"—he smiled his loopy smile—"I could always use a little money."

"I know how you feel." I smiled a bland smile at him. There was a scratching at the door, and he went to let in what turned out to be a very friendly black Labrador.

"Mr. Harriet, I am afraid that it isn't as simple as just signing a check over to you for the money." This was the sales pitch.

"No? Why not, man?" He had sat back down, and the Lab came over and rested his head on Harriet's thigh. The room began to smell of wet dog and coffee. I took a sip, and it was hot and tasted like burnt turpentine.

"Do you mind if I smoke?" I needed something to kill the taste of the coffee and the smell of the dog. I was beginning to wonder if it had rolled in a dead seagull or something.

"No, man, go right ahead. I might have some grass around here . . . you aren't a cop, are you?" He looked at me and raised one eyebrow, and I wasn't sure if he was dense or mocking me. Maybe he was just permanently baked, like a lot of the surviving hippies were.

"No, not for a long time now. Thanks for the grass, but I'll stick to this." I showed him my new pipe, which I began to pack, tamp, light, and re-tamp. The process was laborious, but I was soon rewarded with a fair amount of nice-smelling smoke that helped cut the smell of the dog.

"Mr. Harriet, we are talking about a sum of money that is a little bit over fifteen thousand dollars. The nice, little old lady in question had no close relatives. I am looking for the children of third cousins and things like that. Unfortunately, it isn't always clear who is who and what is what. The lawyer I work for just won't let me give the money away without proving that the recipient is a relative."

"Fifteen thousand dollars. Wow, that is a lot of money. What would you need, like a birth certificate or something?"

"That and I'd have to ask you a few questions. If the answers pan out, then we would go to the lawyer's office, and you could submit a claim."

He took a sip of his coffee and then asked, "What kind of questions, man? I mean, like, personal stuff?" His hippie smile was friendly, but his eyes were like they were in the yard, gauging range.

"No, questions about your parents, where you lived, how long you've been here, that sort of thing."

"Oh, wow . . . um, well, I'm an orphan. I never knew my parents, and I don't have any relatives."

"Oh, um, okay, have you ever lived in Colorado, California, Wyoming, or Nevada?"

"Nope, I lived in Oregon, a little town outside of Eugene, but I moved around chasing jobs. I ended up out here as a caretaker for the Cranberry Company about ten years ago."

"You work for the Cranberry Company? Do they provide this house for you?"

"Yeah, this house is one of the reasons I took the job. They don't pay much. I think they own it or it is part of a lease of theirs."

"Were you ever in the Armed Forces?" This was looking less likely all the time.

"No, man, me? No, I have a heart condition that kept me out of the draft. What do they call it, 4-F? Even if it hadn't, I am not cut out for the army, man. I don't like people telling me what to do. Plus, I am one of those conscious objectors." I didn't correct him. He sipped more of his coffee.

"What about a birth certificate, family papers, or any sort of documents?" I was pretty sure that I knew what the answer was going to be, but sometimes you have to try.

"Gone, man. Lost. I lost everything I had except my driver's license."

"You don't have any relatives on the Cape, do you?"

"I might, but I wouldn't know them. They didn't tell us anything in the orphanage. I might be related to you and not even know it." He smiled again.

"Okay, Mr. Harriet. I should get going. Thanks for your time." I got up and he rose, too.

"Does this mean I don't get any of the money?"

"Probably not. We have to be able to establish that you are related to our client. We can't do that without documentation. That and, based on what you told me, you weren't in any of the places that we know she had relatives. Thanks for the coffee." I stuck my hand out, and he took it.

"No problem, man. I am sorry that I couldn't be more help." He looked sincere.

"No worries." I started to turn away and turned back again. "Say, you don't know a lady named Ruth Silvia, do you?"

"No, should I?" He didn't pause, skip a beat, or look shocked.

"No, I guess not."

"Who is she?"

"She is a distant heir of the estate." I was moving toward the kitchen door. The dog walked over to the door. Harriet opened it for me.

"Hey, man, I am sorry you didn't find what you were looking for."

"Thanks. It just wasn't meant to be."

"What will happen to the money now?"

"Oh, the lawyers and the probate judge will work it out. It doesn't make much difference at this point."

I walked over to the Ghia and got in. She started without protest, and The Band sang about the lights going down on Dixie. I wheeled the car around and watched Harriet in the rearview mirror, watching me from the doorway. He kind of looked like he could be Hammond, but he also looked like a thousand other guys.

He had been my best, last chance, and now it looked pretty much like a dead end. I would have to call Danny and explain that we were absolutely nowhere. Charlie Hammond wasn't on Nantucket, and I didn't have any idea where he was.

When I reached the main road, I turned and headed out of town. I needed to clear my head. I followed Milestone Road out until it ended in the village of Siasconset. 'Sconset was made up of lots of nice houses and lots of small cottages. The nicer houses all dated to the turn of the century, and the smaller fisherman's cottages were even older. The Benchley family had their house somewhere among the older homes, out on the bluff facing the ocean. It was long believed that the Amity Island in *Jaws* was based on Nantucket.

I turned toward Sankaty lighthouse and followed the tight lanes with their high hedges toward the old lighthouse perched on the bluff. When I got there, I parked in the small lot and walked over to the bluff. The chain-link fence with the Coast Guard sign on it rattled and shook in the wind the way a lifelong smoker coughs in the morning. The bluff was high, and the ocean hurled itself onto the sand below with all the fury of the early fall storm that was gripping the island. I looked out at the gray-blue unending vastness of the sea. It was curling in on itself, and there were white caps everywhere. The wind was strong enough to whip into my face, and if it had been coming from my back I would have gone over the bluff.

I never saw who or what did it. One minute I was standing on the bluff wondering if I could get a cigarette lit in the wind, and then the next I heard footsteps rushing in the grass. I started to turn, but it was no use. Something, someone, heavy and solid, crashed into me. I went ass over tea kettle over the bluff's edge.

The U.S. Army has its Airborne School at Fort Benning, Georgia. I, like every other paratrooper in the history of U.S. Army paratroopers, went there. They run you every day, everywhere. Almost immediately, you start practicing the parachute landing fall. The PLF is an almost religious thing at Fort Benning. You practice it all the time. You practice it a lot into giant sandboxes. The sand gets everywhere. It gets in your clothes and your shorts. Paratroopers practice the PLF so much that their sides hurt from landing feet and knees together, falling side of the knee, hip to ass, and then onto your back. Your sides become bruised, and you get sick of doing it. You do it in the pits, you do it from the Swing Landing Trainer, and from the 234-foot tower. The advantage of religiously worshipping at the altar of the PLF is the first time, and every time, you launch out of a plane and your chute opens, you hit the ground hard and PLF. You don't think about it. It is just instinctive.

I was in the air for a second that seemed like twenty long minutes. I hit a lot of sand and rock that was sticking out from the bluff several feet. I did a classic PLF and then rolled the next thirty feet down to the beach. I lay on the beach, listening to the waves and waiting for my body to start breathing again. It did. I hurt, but nothing was broken. Somehow my Colt was still in its shoulder holster. I looked up, but there was no one up on the bluff. I brushed off as much of the wet sand as I could. I had gotten lucky that there had been a collapse and some sand and rocks were sticking out.

I got up. There was no way I was going to climb up the bluff I had just been pushed off of. I looked left and then right and turned toward Codfish Park. I could walk back to the Ghia on the only road I was familiar with. Walking back to the car, I thought about who might have pushed me off of the bluff. The problem was it could be anyone. After the walk, my head was clear and the Ghia was where I left her. I didn't need the keys; the door was unlocked. Everything was where it should be, and the car was unmolested. I got in the Ghia, started her, and steered her toward town, toward the hotel and the phone. I was driving back closer to Danny and to reality.

Chapter 18

I followed the road back into town and parked in the hotel lot. My room had been cleaned, and there were more messages to call Danny. I took off my coat and poured a slug of whiskey from the bottle. I settled into a chair with the whiskey, my notebook, a cigarette, and the phone. I dialed Danny in Boston and waited on hold, listening to the wind as it whipped outside. Danny came on and was only a little less harsh than the wind.

"Please tell me you have something." It was more of a command than a question.

"I met the guy. The age is right. In all honesty, I can't tell much from the picture." It was hard to tell much from a grainy thirty-year-old picture of a young man in Marine Corps dress blues.

"What did he say?" Danny wasn't a fountain of patience.

"Not much. I didn't come right out and ask him if he was Charles Hammond, who had deserted his wife and child almost thirty years ago." I took a sip of the whiskey and felt it slide down into the center of me.

"What, did you give him some bullshit story about an inheritance?" Danny sounded a little disgusted, and I felt my face flush.

"You know, counselor, I don't ask about how you defend your clients, so don't question me about how I do my job."

"Okay, okay, killer, so what did he say?"

"Nothing. The guy I spoke to is an aging hippie out here just dropping out of life. That being said, let me give you some information so that you can have some dirty cop make a little money getting it for you."

"Hey, come on, you used to get me information, but no one could accuse you of being dirty." He sounded almost sincere; then I remembered he was a criminal defense attorney.

"Yeah, but I did that because we were friends, and back then you didn't have two nickels to rub together. I knew you before you were trying so hard to be respectable. I need you to check a name and a license plate for me."

"Isn't that your job? What am I paying you for?"

"I can check on it, but you can get it done a little faster than I can. I know that you are in a hurry to get results."

"Okay, tell me." I told him Harriet's name and gave him the plate number to the pickup. He said that he would call me back in a couple of hours. He hung up, and I didn't bother to tell him about the incident on the bluff. He paid me to take risks. He didn't need to hear about all of them.

I got up and went to my bag and pulled out the legal pad with my case notes on it, the folder from Pinkerton, a fresh legal pad, and two felt tip pens. I managed to tuck all of it into a brown paper bag. I put on my coat and headed back out into the wind and rain.

The local library was actually the Nantucket Athenaeum. It turned out to be a handsome Greek Revival building with broad steps, big doors, and white Doric columns, across from the post office. If the outside of the building made me feel small, the inside made me feel welcome. In front, at the far end of the building was a large desk/counter affair, with a suitably matronly woman in her sixties behind it. She looked at me as if I had tracked in a smelly dog turd.

To my right were rows of books, and to my left was what I had come for, the reading area. Rows of small partitioned desks and hard wooden captain's chairs in front of them. A few of them were occupied by old men reading newspapers. I sat down behind an unoccupied desk and took out the folder, my case notes, and the fresh legal pad. I went through it all slowly, taking notes as I went, drawing and redrawing the timeline. I was trying to make the pieces of the jigsaw puzzle fit, and I wasn't sure that I wasn't forcing pieces into place. Occasionally I would take a break to go out and smoke a cigarette on the wide front steps or walk around in the small, attractive park attached to the Athenaeum.

I finished up my work knowing that I was no closer to finding Charlie Hammond than when I had started. In fact, I was certain that he wasn't on Nantucket Island and that I was wasting my client's money. Why had someone pushed me off of the bluff? It could have nothing to do with the case. I went back to the hotel so that I could hear as much from Danny. He called fifteen minutes after he said he would, and he was terse at best. The truck was registered to the Cranberry Company. Harriet had gotten a Massachusetts driver's license ten or eleven years earlier. There was nothing on paper for him before that in the Commonwealth. He had a couple of vagrancy charges from the western states but otherwise no record.

I was not sure what I had been hoping for, but Danny was succinct and explicit when he said, "There is nothing going on out there. Get your ass back here and stop wasting our client's money." He didn't sound happy, but I wasn't sure that I could blame him. He was going to have to explain to his client how I had gone on a vacation on her dime. Most private detectives have cases that don't come to a neat, end-of-the-TV-show-hour conclusion. Missing persons cases are usually the ones that don't. Sometimes they don't get resolved. They are almost as bad as when someone hires you to look into a homicide that happened years ago. Time is the detective's enemy; the more time that has passed, the less likely one is to solve a case. Knowing these things doesn't make the failures any easier to take.

"I'll get the next ferry to the mainland. There has been a pretty big storm out here, so things might be backed up."

"All right, just don't have too extravagant a vacation on the Swift expense account." He sounded more uptight every time I talked to him.

"No, I won't. Danny, I really thought I had a lead that the Pinkerton boys didn't. You know, a shot at solving this thing."

"Andy, you know better than I do that sometimes leads dead end, that trails go cold, and that cases don't get solved. You gave it your best shot, and that is all that matters." He knew I hated losing.

"Okay, I'll be home tomorrow or the next day. It all depends on a boat at this point." Saying it tasted like vinegar and ashes in my mouth.

"Come into the office when you get back and I will settle your bill. On the plus side, if you and Pinkerton can't find her father, then he doesn't exist. If he doesn't exist, then there is no scandal waiting to happen."

"True. Still, I would like to think that I could have found him. Fuck. This was a pretty thin lead." I took another sip of whiskey, shook a Player's out of the box, and lit it. The smoke worked its way into my lungs, sending off chain reactions in my body. It had been a pretty thin lead, but I was sure that it was going somewhere.

"Andy, don't worry about it. You tried your best. Now come home." He hung up, and I finished my drink and my smoke listening to the wind howling outside. I still hadn't bothered to tell him about getting pushed off the bluff. Now it almost didn't seem real.

I spent another hour and a half going through my notes and the Pinkerton folder. I went through it beginning to end and back again. In the end, I was no closer to finding Charlie Hammond. When I couldn't take much more of it, I decided to get cleaned up for dinner. I showered and dressed in my normal clothes: jeans, white button-down, and corduroy blazer. The Colt .32 went back in its shoulder holster, and the parka was now dry. My beard and my hair were as neat as either could be. It had taken a Herculean effort to get the sand out of my hair.

I walked out the door of the hotel and down the steps. The wind whipped around and pulled at me. I could hear the branches of the large elms moving and swaying, and wondered if I would hear them crack. The weather suited my mood. The wind was slapping wet leaves against every surface that would hold them. I wound my way through the old, sometimes cobbled streets of the quaint New England island, former whaling capital of the world, until I arrived at Shelly's apartment. I went up the wet, slippery steps and knocked on the door.

She opened the door and ushered me in. "Hiya, Tomcat." She held her face up to be kissed, and I was not one to say no. She was wearing a long peasant skirt, with low-heeled riding boots and a denim work shirt. Peasant chic. Her hair was in a ponytail, and she smelled softly of lilacs. "Are you hungry, Tomcat?" She was smiling and pulling on a sheepskin coat.

"I could eat. What do you have in mind?" I enjoyed watching the way that she moved; she was comfortable in her body in a way that spoke of high school cheerleading or dance lessons. She would hitch her shoulders when she thought I wasn't looking.

"You are going to take me out to a place called The Club Car."

"I am indeed. Why is it called The Club Car?"

"There used to be a steam railroad out here about a hundred years ago. It ran from town to 'Sconset. It folded when cars became commonplace. The old club car is literally attached to the restaurant. It is now the bar, and there is a charming old rogue who plays the piano and sings raunchy old songs."

"It sounds like my kind of place. How is the food?"

"Pretty good, but we are mostly going for the bar and the raunchy songs."

"I would expect nothing less."

We left her place and walked down the steps. We walked down the alleyway that made up Old North Wharf. The wind was just as fierce, and describing the night as raw just didn't seem to do it justice. I understood why she had chosen a sheepskin coat. We were walking arm in arm, and it felt nice. It had been a long time since I had walked anywhere with a woman walking pressed up against me for warmth and companionship. We turned onto Easy Street, and the wind snatched at us, whipping wet leaves and generally reminding us of how small we were.

We stepped out of the rain and the wind into a world of warmth and soft light. The restaurant was nice, with a dozen or so tables with white linen tablecloths. One wall had a few large booths. Every table had a tea candle in a glass chimney providing a soft pool of light. There was a door to the left that led to the old club car. The hostess came and led us to a small table by a window.

"It is a mess out there." I was master of the obvious.

"I know. It looks bad. The ferry probably won't run tomorrow if it keeps up like this." She was looking out the window and watching the leaves blow by.

"That is good." She looked at me and raised an eyebrow. "I didn't find the man I was looking for. My client's lawyer wants me to go back to Boston as soon as possible. He told me to stop vacationing on his client's dime."

"Tomcat, I thought you were making up some story about being a detective. You really are one, aren't you?" She was looking at me with large, round eyes.

"I am, but not a very good one, according to the lawyer." I could hear Danny's voice in my head telling me not to vacation on the Swifts' money.

"He sounds like an asshole."

"He is. He is also one of my oldest friends, but that doesn't mean he isn't an asshole." She laughed, and it was nice to hear.

"Tell me more about him."

"Danny . . . well, Danny and I grew up together in South Boston. Southie."

"Is it a nice place with brick streets and bookstores?"

"No, that is Back Bay. Southie . . . is one of the places that is made up of three-family tenements—generations live in them, assigned floors by age. You had reached the pinnacle of your earning potential and age by the time you moved into the first floor. You also couldn't walk up to the third floor anymore, which you had moved into when you got married.

"Our part of the neighborhood was a little poorer, a little meaner, and a little more run-down. At some point,

someone had gone around selling siding in our neighborhood. It was tar paper on one side and on the other, it
looked like brick. Fake brick. Where we grew up, brick
houses were for people who had good jobs, education. Every
other house ended up with the tar-paper brick. Have you
ever seen a three-family with a porch on every floor made
of brick? Of course not. It looked good for about a year,
and the brick-looking part started to peel. Then it just
looked like shit with fake brick stuck to it.

"In our neighborhood, you worked in the mills back
when there was work, or the shipyards. Lucky people got
jobs with the post office or became teachers, priests, or
nurses. The few doctors and lawyers the neighborhood
makes move out to the suburbs. The gangsters stay, like
some sort of run-down royalty in nylon Celtics team jack-
ets. Most of the men die young, and most of the women
live long after they're gone.

"There is a bar on every corner and a package store, a
packie, selling liquor, smokes, and Lotto tickets every few
blocks. Most days after work, the men would stop in their
favorite bar for a boilermaker or two. Friday and Satur-
days, they drink away most of their pay, go home and
fight with their wives, and Sunday is the Lord's Day. Family dinner after church and watching football on the TV.
Most of us went to Catholic school, and the kids from big
families wore hand-me-downs that were still considered
new when the third kid got them. It was poor, and it was
depressing. It was mostly shanty Irish."

"Shanty Irish, as opposed to?"

"Lace curtain Irish . . . those are the ones who make it
up the ladder. The ones who become lawyers or doctors.
They leave and move to the suburbs and join the country
club. Lace curtain Irish are the ones who end up in brick
houses or at least single-family ones. They live in nice

neighborhoods, and their kids don't have to wear hand-me-downs. They buy new cars and vote Republican, because they stopped giving a fuck about the most Irish saint of all . . . JFK.

"Danny and I were shanty Irish. My dad worked as a bookkeeper for the sugar company. He was a sweet man who loved poetry and whiskey. Mom was his German war bride. She split when I was six. My dad wrote and drank more. For all of his disappointment and drinking, I don't think he ever hit me. A rarity in a place where slapping a child was considered liberal parenting.

"Growing up half-Kraut meant I was always the Indian in Cowboys and Indians. I got in a lot of fights. I lost a lot of them. Veteran's Day was like running the gauntlet. My dad's drinking and perpetually broken heart meant we were poor. But he had books. He loved books, and I was always reading. The library was the safest, nicest place I had ever been in.

"Danny grew up next door. He was skinny and bad at sports. My dad was a sad drunk. Danny's dad was a mean one. My dad never hit me; Danny's was an artist with the belt. One summer at the local swimming pool, Danny had so many bruises on his pale Irish skin that he looked like a bag of Wonder Bread.

"The same kids who liked using me as a punching bag because I was half-Kraut loved doing the same to Danny because he was smart and skinny. Danny got it at home from his dad and then again in school. One day I took a swing at one of the Murphy brothers who was picking on Danny. We have been friends ever since.

"We were in a race to leave Southie. Danny was being suffocated by it. He wasn't going to work in the shipyards or the mills. He wasn't going into the church, and that would have just left the mob. Not Danny. We both got into colleges. Danny stayed and became a lawyer and left the neighborhood."

"What made you want to leave?"

"I knew the world was bigger than our few blocks of the neighborhood. I never fit in, never felt at home. I felt like I spoke the language, but that I wasn't fluent. I was missing out on nuances and was always out of step with everyone else.

"Then Vietnam came. I wasn't doing well in college and, like lots of other young men going back centuries, I heard the drumbeat and bugle call. Flunking out of college would have meant moving back to Southie. A job in a factory if I was lucky. Going to the same bar for boilermakers every night after work. Nope, not for me. I would have blown my brains out.

"Me, Vietnam saved me. The army let me travel, exposed me to different people and ideas. In Vietnam, I found work that I was good at and loved. Then the cops and now this. In the end, we both got out. Me, I am still trying to figure out what the hell I am doing. Danny is trying to put as much distance between him and the skinny kid in Southie as he can."

I didn't tell her that Danny's ticket out involved some very scary mob people. That they paid well, but that Danny was always on call. Danny had excused himself from more than one family dinner in order to go bail out a guy who another guy called Danny about. Danny spent much of his work life fixing problems and bringing stacks of cash from one guy to another. Danny was the keeper of their secrets and arranged everything that they did that was legal or near legal. He had set up corporations and businesses that washed money. He had found places to put money, on and offshore. Danny had gotten murderers, pimps, drug dealers, and rapists out of prison. Danny kept their soldiers safe and the bosses safer. There was no denying he was valuable to them, and that meant he wasn't free. I could see why he was hoping Deborah Swift would be his next big client. She might be another step farther from Southie.

The waiter brought us our menus, and we ordered. We split an order of scallops wrapped in bacon. She ordered roast chicken with rosemary and new potatoes. I ordered paella. I am nuts about paella. We split a bottle of California chardonnay that was not as special as its price would lead you to believe. The meal was good and, as usual, the waiters and waitresses all seemed to know her.

"So, you are really a private investigator?"

"Yep."

"Just like Magnum P.I.?"

"No, I am not that tall. More like Philip Marlowe or Sam Spade. Don't let my hippie hair fool you."

"Do you carry a gun?" She leaned forward and used a stage whisper. There was a little more than a hint of cleavage, and I could smell lilacs.

"Yes, I do."

"All the time?"

"Not in the shower or at the beach." I hadn't been to the beach since some in-country R&R in Da Nang . . . we brought our guns to the beach. I didn't like Wollaston Beach, and I couldn't afford the Cape and islands in the summer. Plus, my pale Irish flesh burns fast in the summer sun and my scars show. I don't mind the sunburn.

"Do you have one now?" She had lost the stage whisper, and I squirmed uncomfortably in my chair.

"Yes." I was uncomfortable with such honesty.

"Why? Do you think that Nantucket is so dangerous?"

"No, I don't think Nantucket is that dangerous." On the other hand, I did get pushed off of a bluff this afternoon.

"Okay, why?"

"I grew up in Southie, which was tough, but most things could be settled with our fists. If things were really bad, a bike chain, stick, or knife. When I went to Vietnam, the little brown men were trying to kill me. I respected their prowess. They had spent centuries trying to kill the Chinese, then the Japanese, then the French, and then the Americans. When I showed up, they had been fighting for centuries before there was an America, and they were pretty good at killing foreigners.

"I worked in a dangerous part of a dangerous, stupid war. In our corner of it, they threw their best men at us; they put bounties on our heads. They were not to be taken lightly. A very, very skilled enemy was trying very hard to kill me. I respected their professionalism.

"When I came home, I was more scared just trying to be a normal person, going to college and trying to fit in, than I ever was in Vietnam. Home was chaos. In the war, there had been an order to it. Things made sense. Everything we did, everything they did was done for a reason.

"Then I joined the cops. That was true chaos. People weren't trying to kill like the NVA—they didn't have the skill—but death was so common and random and casual. There were so many ways to get killed in the cops . . . so many of them random. Car accidents, family disputes, convicts who don't want to go back, drug dealers, murderers, rapists, crazies, knives, guns, straight razors, baseball bats, and all sorts of other random shit.

"Now I am a private license, off on my own. No artillery and air support. No backup. No boys in blue with nightsticks. Out in the world where people still want to hurt me; it is just me, so I carry a gun."

She leaned back and looked at me for a long minute. She then picked up her wine and had a sip; every move was slow and deliberate and made me ache a little in the very center of myself. I watched her throat work as she swallowed and thought about the night before, kissing the hollow of her neck right where it met her jawbone. She put the glass down, and her eyes seemed to sparkle and dance in the candlelight.

"Ohh, Tomcat, you are soooo serious. I don't like guns, but I do like you." Her smile was what I was growing accustomed to, slightly mocking, with little, pearl-like teeth.

We finished our dinner and decided that dessert would be best in the bar, the old club car itself, in the form of cocktails. I slid a bunch of Mrs. Swift's twenty-dollar bills in the leather case with the check. We got up and went to the old club car. She walked ahead of me, and I followed. Her ponytail swayed as she walked, and when she walked, it was all hips and shapely bottom. I probably would have followed her anywhere. If I was less of a gentleman, I would have goosed her, and if I were more of one, I wouldn't have stared so much.

The actual club car itself was narrow and tight. One half of it, the half abutting the restaurant, was made of the bar, with a small cutout for an upright piano, which was being played by a thin, ginger-haired man in his early sixties. He was singing, not the usual jazz piano standards, but songs from my father's war. We ordered drinks and sat at one of the small tables opposite the bar, next to the windows of the old club car, which looked out at the building next door.

The man playing piano was wearing a pearl-gray suit that spoke of English tailoring, good breeding, good schools, and money. It also spoke of a style that hadn't been popular since a time when men wore hats outside. He had a neatly trimmed beard that hugged his jaw. A slow parade of scotch and sodas made their way to the piano and back again, but he never seemed to get drunk. He was

American but spoke the Queen's English. The type who said "boot" and "bonnet" instead of "trunk" and "hood," and believed that serving tea in a mug was a form of sacrilege.

He was a good piano player, but more the talented amateur with good lessons than the classically trained, concert pianist type. He should have been in Rick's Café Américain or in some bar in London during the Blitz instead of a bar on Nantucket. He certainly played better than I ever would.

"That's Scotty. He has been here for years." She said it over the rim of her Manhattan.

"I like what he plays. He isn't local?" This was said over the rim of my own scotch and soda.

"No, he is from New York but has been playing out here forever. When the tourist season ends, he goes back to Manhattan. He comes back for closing weekend."

"Everyone knows everything about everyone here?"

"Yes, that is why we don't have any private eyes of our own out here. No money in it."

"I can see that. I didn't get too far out here."

"Maybe not, but you did get to me, Tomcat. Isn't that worth the trip?" She was teasing me again.

"Of course, and then some. I just don't like being wrong or not finding the guy I am supposed to. It is some sort of professional pride."

"Or male ego, tough guys don't like striking out?"

"Or not so tough guy, in my case. I can't deny the male ego thing, but mostly I just like to get results for my clients. I don't want to be the private investigator who can't find people."

"No, I can see where that would be bad for business. On the other hand, could anyone else have found him?" Her eyes were big and earnest, and I felt old.

"Others tried and didn't get too far, either. I thought

that I had been cleverer than them. I thought that an ob-
scure lead led me to him out here. Instead, I just bent the
facts into something that fit my theory."

"Everyone does that. If people didn't, then no one would
ever discover anything new. No one would try to climb moun-
tains or go to the moon." She put her little, unblemished hand
over my rougher, scarred one. "The Earth was flat until
someone looked at the facts and bent them to their theory,
and the Earth became a sphere. I assume you followed the
facts and your hunch, your theory, as far as they could be
taken. That is what your client was paying you for."

"Okay, okay. You are right. Let's not talk about this
anymore." Failure is still failure, and I hate to fail. I find it
hard to be philosophical about it. I went to the bar and ordered us two more cocktails. Scotty was singing a dirty
song about Hitler's underwear and Göring's boots and
Churchill's cigar. Most of the crowd was too young to get
most of the references, but Scotty sang the dirty parts with
gusto, and the crowd played along. The drinks came, and
I put more of Mrs. Swift's money on the bar. I wanted to
hear The Doors or The Rolling Stones or something other
than my father's music. I carried our cocktails to our little
table and sat down.

"Tomcat, you brought me another drink. You are trying
to get me drunk and have your way with me." Her nose
was wrinkled, and her smile was as crooked as ever.

"You are right about that." I smiled, and it was pretty
crooked, too.

"Silly, Tomcat, you don't even have to get me drunk to
do that." She said it and somehow, without leaving her
chair or moving too much, she shimmied in her seat. It
was a shimmy that spoke of hips and breasts and of all
things good and true.

"Well, I don't mind buying you a drink." We drank in

companionable silence for a while. When we did talk, it was about nothing in particular. Not small talk, just not the type of conversation that would last in either of our memories.

"So, what now, you go back to the mainland and go on looking for this guy?"

"No, I have pretty much hit a dead end."

"Now what? Another case like this one—travel, sex, adventure, and glamour?"

I laughed a little. "No, most of my cases aren't like this at all."

She arched an eyebrow. "What are they like?"

"Most of the time I work divorce cases; you know, waiting to catch someone's husband or wife cheating, and taking pictures. They are in my office paying me good money. They already know, they just want me to confirm it. Or I work insurance fraud cases."

"Insurance fraud?"

"Yeah, someone claims to be injured on the job. Makes a workers' comp claim, and I get sent to take pictures of them running a marathon or skydiving, or catch them doing things that they couldn't do if they were really hurt. Once in a blue moon, the fraud is about something that someone is claiming to be lost, destroyed, or stolen, so they can collect the insurance payout. Usually it is workers' comp. Once in a while I get a missing persons case, but, for the most part, it is a lot of long, boring hours."

"It sounds seedy." She wrinkled her nose a little.

"It is seedy, but I have to eat." The truth is, I liked the freedom, being my own boss and making my own hours. I didn't mind cold, stiff hours sitting in a car, watching and waiting. I loved the occasional interesting case that came my way, and I loved just being in the game.

Then it was time to go, which in this case involved her having to stop and say goodbye to a fair amount of people. Saying good-bye involved her hugging a lot and my standing awkwardly off to one side. We got near the door, and I helped her on with her coat and shrugged into my own. Outside, the wind was still blowing, and it was still cold. We managed to stop in a few doorways to steal kisses on the way back to her apartment. It was nice, nice in a way that I had forgotten about. We made our way up the stairs to her apartment, and inside we ended up on the couch in a brief, urgent, passionate struggle.

Afterward, I lit the fire, and she lit a joint. We shared the joint, bourbon, and each other's warmth. Somewhere, somehow our clothes ended up in heaps and piles around her living room. Outside, the wind shrieked and howled, and inside it was warm. I could smell sex and pot and felt mellow by the fire. She was sitting behind me, tracing lazy circles on my back.

"Tomcat, this is nice."

"Yes, it is. When I was in Nam, this is exactly what I thought about when I thought about coming home."

"Tomcat, you know how to make a girl feel good about herself." She pulled my face to hers, and we kissed. Her fingers started to probe my new, darkening bruises.

"These are new. What were you doing this afternoon?"

"Um, someone pushed me off of the bluff by the lighthouse."

"Sankaty Light? Who would do that?"

"I have no idea. Do you have a jealous boyfriend?"

"Um, I do have an ex . . . but I can't picture him doing anything like that."

"Don't worry about it. There must be better things for us to talk about."

She showed me that I was right. We ended up spending the night on the couch, making love and sleeping and waking up to make love again.

I woke up with a headache that reminded me that I

couldn't drink like I could ten years ago. The bright, painful shaft of sunlight in my eye didn't help, either. I was stiff and sore and felt as though I had been worked over with a lead pipe. I heard someone groan and realized it was me. I managed to ease myself into a sitting position and would have shot myself except I was pretty sure that a gunshot would only make my head hurt worse. I lit my first cigarette and coughed as it burned my lungs. Shelly padded in from the kitchen wearing my shirt and handed me a glass of tomato juice.

"Here, Tomcat, this will help you feel better."

"I doubt it, but thanks." I gagged it down and barely contained the revolt in my stomach.

"I called. The ferry is running and you should be able to leave on the noon boat." Her face was serious.

"Are you eager to get rid of me?"

"No, Tomcat. If you were the type who could get used to living in a house, I would take you in in a heartbeat. But we both know that you aren't the type who can stay in one place for long. You are an old alley cat, and pretty soon you'd be looking for a way out." She was smiling, but it was a little brittle, like fall sunshine in the late afternoon.

"I do have my flaws."

"Don't we all." She brushed the hair out of her eyes.

"Do you ever get up to Boston?"

"I do."

"You could call me. They have restaurants and bars." I started to look for my pants.

"Or you could call me . . ." She was biting her lower lip.

"I need your number."

"Hold on." She left the room. I pulled on my pants and socks and shivered. She came back wearing a sweatshirt and handed me my shirt, which I put on. She went to one of the boxes in the corner and pulled out a flyer advertising one of the gallery shows. She wrote on it in ballpoint pen and handed it to me.

"Don't you need this for work?" I said, waving the flyer at her.

"Oh, those, no, they were extra from an older show. We ordered too many. I should throw them away, but I can't bring myself to. Now they have a use. You will remember me and know where to find me."

"Clever girl."

She had written her full name and number on a glossy trifold brochure for the show. I put it in my pocket. My head ached too much to look too closely at anything that wasn't an Anacin. I got dressed, and we kissed and said our goodbyes with minimal fuss.

Outside, last night's fierce wind was a gentle breeze that ruffled my hair. The sun was bright and hurt my hungover eyes, making me wish that I hadn't left my sunglasses in the room. I walked back to the hotel, stopping at The Steamship Authority. A nice lady there was able to get me a standby reservation, assuring me that my spot was low enough that I should be able to get on the noon boat.

I walked back up the hill to the Jared Coffin House. I smoked a Player's on the way, feeling a little better but not ready for food. I stopped at the desk to collect my bill, conscious of smelling like a night on the town and aware of the matronly desk clerk's disapproving look. Why book a hotel room and stay out all night? I took a hot shower, turning the water cold for as long as I could stand it. I dressed, packed, and went down to settle my bill. The Ghia started, but under protest after all of that rain. I drove around the island and then back to The Steamship Authority. The woman was right; I did make it on.

I parked and went up on deck to smoke my pipe and watch the island as the ferry pulled out. The gulls were turning in the sky above and around the boat, but there was nothing to feed them. From the deck, I could see Shelly's apartment. I imagined I could see her curled up on the couch by the fire. I could almost picture myself there next to her.

The ferry began to pull away from the slip, and I could see an old Dodge pickup truck with a wooden frame driving up Broad Street, away from the ferry as it pulled out. I watched it as it grew smaller and smaller, then turned and was gone. My theory about Ed Harriet and Charlie Hammond was growing smaller and smaller, until it was gone.

Chapter 19

The drive home was a morose affair. There was nothing good on the radio, the sun was in my eyes, the taste of defeat was bitter in my mouth, and I got caught in traffic. The traffic in Boston was bad enough to make me wonder if I couldn't walk into the city faster. I detoured through Chinatown for takeout and made it back to Back Bay by the time my stomach was rumbling.

I spent the evening sitting at the kitchen table eating Chinese food, drinking Löwenbräu, and reviewing my case notes. I rewrote and consolidated my case notes on a yellow legal pad. It was a long summary of a short failure.

I would send them out to the service that would type them up. I had an IBM electric typewriter, but for clients I used a professional service. It didn't cost much, and it made an impression. I worked through what was left of the pack of Player's and couldn't help but feel that I had been on some expensive fool's errand.

When I finished, I stood up and stretched out my back, which was stiff from being hunched over the table for hours. I neatened the table and went to find a glass, ice, and the bottle of scotch. I found *The Raymond Chandler Omnibus* and turned on the local radio station that played jazz at night. Nina Simone sang to me, the scotch warmed me, and I was able to let Chandler transport me to the exotic world of 1940s Los Angeles. Philip Marlowe made it all look so easy. In his sun-dappled, rain-soaked Los Angeles, there were beautiful dames, glib lines, and a man who knew how to take a punch. In the end, Marlowe always figured out the case and got the bad guy. I was no Marlowe. I was more like a private version of Inspector Clouseau.

I drank and read and must have fallen asleep. I woke up to the sound of birds singing from my radio. The local station had switched over to its classical music programming. A deep voice came out of the speaker telling me about Handel. I switched the thing off and went to shower.

A hot shower and a couple of cups of strong black coffee didn't do much to make me feel better. I put my case notes in a folder and put the final draft in an envelope. I put the Colt in its holster under my arm and set out for the office. My office wasn't far, and the morning was crisp and sunny. I stopped at the typists' to drop off my notes, which they said they would have done late that afternoon. They charged extra for the rush. I picked up my other jobs from them—a divorce and two workers' comp cases—paid them for everything and walked two more blocks to my office.

My office was a two-room affair in a five-story building. I was above a pizza place, facing out over a busy street. All day long I could smell dough, pepperoni, and sausage cooking. The door was half-frosted glass with my name and profession on it in gold paint. The front room was taken up by a couch and two chairs that I had gotten at the Salvation Army and lots of filing cabinets. The inner room was my office proper. It had an old wooden desk with a squeaky wooden office chair, two wooden chairs in front of the desk, and filing cabinets along one wall. On the other side of the room was an old safe the same height as the filing cabinets but twice as wide. It had come with the office as a leftover from some business that had been here for years. Over time, the businesses had come and gone, but no one wanted to move the big, heavy safe, and it sat, as it always had. I kept it for show. It made the clients think that their cases were safe in the big safe. A locksmith friend of mine had been able to open it and reset the combination for me.

The desk had a banker's lamp on it and a black telephone. Built into the desk, where there used to be a place for a typewriter stand, was a small safe. In the safe I usually kept my checkbook, some keys, some private notes, and a heavy Ruger .357 Magnum revolver. It was big, with a four-inch barrel, and was just too heavy to carry. I kept it for those times when angry ex-husbands or paramours came by looking to settle some sort of score.

The office was dusty and the air was stale. I opened the window a few inches to let out the stale air. I could hear the street noises—traffic, horns, and somewhere far off a jackhammer was pounding away its staccato beat. I took out my newly acquired pipe, packed the bowl, and lit it. I sat puffing it into life, watching the people wander by outside. Some went into the coffee shop across the street, others just moved on through the crowds. That was one of the advantages of being self-employed: I could smoke my pipe in my office and watch people walking around outside.

I typed up and sent out a few bills to clients. They had not been interesting cases, and the only travel involved had been to places in and around Boston. It had been the usual tour of cheating spouses and workers' compensation fraud cases. When that was done, I took out the checkbook and sent money to the bill collectors. In between, I nursed, cajoled, and relit my pipe half a dozen times. I was definitely new to it and still hadn't figured out what I was doing.

At lunchtime, I went downstairs to Marconi's for a bite. The old man liked me and would never let me eat reheated pizza. He usually fed me what he had going on in the kitchen. Today it was mushroom risotto with sausage made from wild boar. I heard that he harvested the wild mushrooms himself from a hidden location somewhere in New England. Some people had said that he went north to Vermont or New Hampshire. Others said he went to Providence, Rhode Island, to Roger Williams Park, where he had a secret spot. Either way, they were fantastic. The sausage was an even greater secret. I only know that it was homemade and was not shy about garlic.

The old man was there and made me an espresso with a machine that he brought over from Italy. When I came in in the morning, he made me a cappuccino, but later in the day it was always espresso. On really cold days or days when I looked like I had been through it, he made me a *Correctto* with a shot of sambuca in it.

After lunch, I went back upstairs and spent time watching the comings and goings on the street below. I watched the owner in the market next to the coffee shop chase out some kids who were no doubt helping themselves to some candy. I watched people in business clothes walk by, moving without ever looking at anyone. I saw the bum sitting over the grate, catching some warm air and holding out a cup. No one gave him much, but it didn't seem like he expected anything.

When I got bored of trying my hand at keeping the pipe ... and waiting for the phone to ring, I went downstairs and across the street to the market. I took a *Globe* and an apple. I left him a handful of coins, and we wasted a few minutes talking about the Patriots. Then I went back up-stairs to wait. Wait for the phone to ring. I knew that I was going to be summoned by Danny. He was waiting for my final bill. Over the years, we hadn't bothered with the mail, secretaries, or offices. He would call, and we would meet in some bar or restaurant. We did our business over cigarettes and meals. We talked cases and reminisced. I knew him well enough to know that he was pissed about my coming up empty-handed. It wasn't so much that it didn't happen. Sometimes there isn't any resolution. The missing person can't be found, or fraud can't be proved, or spouses aren't cheating.

What was going to piss Danny off was that Deborah Swift was a big name. She could steer a lot of business his way. She could do a lot of business. Danny didn't need the money. His regular client base of mobsters, both Italian and Irish, were paying through the nose. He also had a steady clientele of robbers, con men, rapists, loan sharks, and drug dealers. Danny didn't need new clients for their money. He was rolling in it. Some part of Danny wanted to have respectable clients. He wanted to have the type of clients, to be the type of lawyer whom his lace curtain Irish wife and her family could be proud of. Danny wanted that respectability badly.

He called at four and told me the name of a bar that we both liked. We didn't have a regular place. Danny tried to keep our show on the road so as to minimize his col-leagues seeing him out too often. I didn't care either way. Danny had the cunning of an old jungle fighter, but he worked with lawyers, and they are a ruthless bunch.

I read the paper to kill time. There wasn't much of in-terest on the international front, and the city news was bad. There was a one paragraph blurb in the regional news about a fire on the Cape. Ruth Silvia was killed when her house burned down in the night. The police and fire department said that it appeared accidental and ruled out foul play. They said there was evidence that she had been smoking in bed. Ruth Silvia smoking in bed . . . probably for the last fifty years. Her paintings would now go up in value, and it seemed that a large piece of Cape Cod was going to become available for development, because, according to the *Globe*, she didn't have any living relatives. More proof of my wild-goose chase.

Something about all of it was bothering me. I just couldn't put together what it was. Was it coincidence that just days after I visited her that her farm burned down and she was dead? Did it have anything to do with her talking to me? She had all the weed at her house, was it a competitor? Why? I couldn't see the percentage in killing an old hippie painter. I could see the percentage in killing her and stealing all that weed.

Were her paintings worth anything? Was she a forger? Her stuff looked a lot like O'Keeffe's. The most likely reason was the pot. Unless she was tied up in some art racket. Maybe a private detective sniffing around had made someone nervous. Nervous enough to kill her? I was getting ahead of myself; so far, the fire was deemed accidental. I could head out there and take a look. Arson leaves marks.

I left at half past three for the twenty-minute walk to the bar. The sun was still out, and the wind wasn't bad. For the most part, Boston is a walkable city. The area I live and work in is made up of old brick buildings, none of which is too tall, and certainly not someone's idea of an essay in architectural experimentation. When they built the John Hancock building, everyone complained about how the glass was going to ruin the look and feel of old

Boston. What no one counted on was the glass reflecting the proud old buildings in the proud old city.

The bar was not far from the Common but not near it, either. It was half-full with the slip-out-of-work-to-drink crowd, which was better than the I-started-at-lunch-and-never-stopped crowd. Also, knowing Danny, he was the only member of the local Bar Association in the place. He liked to polish his veneer of respectability more than a housewife with antique furniture in the front room.

His suit was a three-piece blue pinstripe from Brooks Brothers that seemed to accentuate his slight but growing paunch. I sat next to him at the bar, and he turned to look at me. He had a glass of some sort of scotch, and the bartender brought me a Löwenbräu when asked. When the bartender had moved off to dry some glasses with a rag, Danny turned to face me. "How am I going to explain to the client that I very dearly want to keep, that you, the investigator that I recommended, not only didn't find anything but went on an all-expense paid vacation courtesy of her checkbook?"

"Tell her I followed a lead and it didn't pan out. Sometimes cases like this don't go anywhere."

"That is what you want me to tell her? Bullshit! You milked this one." Danny's voice crept up a little.

"Danny, this isn't like some TV show. The case isn't wrapped up in an hour after a word from our sponsors. The only other thing I could do is waste more of her money by going to every address that he ever lived at and seeing if anyone there remembers him. That would be a huge waste of time and money."

"Considering Pinkerton has already done all of that, I agree. That doesn't solve my problem of trying to explain to her that we spent a lot of her money to tell her what she already knows. I don't know if I made this clear, but cultivating her as a client is important to me." His voice was just a notch south of accusatory. It was almost impossible to explain to a client that sometimes the case doesn't turn out the way they want it to.

"Tell her your investigator did his job and that he didn't find anything. Her father disappeared and doesn't seem likely to reappear anytime soon. Tell her she got her money's worth."

"That is what you call it? You lark off to Nantucket and probably shacked up with some broad and had a great time, and you don't have a thing to show for it. This is typical." I had known Danny forever, and this wasn't like him.

"Typical? Typical of what?" I was not enjoying his tone of voice. We were now a couple of drinks in and both feeling our Irish or, in my case, half-Irish.

"You have been a flake ever since Nam. You couldn't stay in college, you couldn't stay with the cops, you only take easy cases, workers' comp, divorce work . . . you could have gone far with the cops, gone far, been a lawyer, anything." Now he was sounding like the mother I never had.

"Lawyer . . . fuck you. I might be a keyhole peeper, but there are some things I won't do for money."

He threw a punch at me. Actually, he did punch me. It glanced off my chin and knocked me off my barstool onto my feet. It wasn't much of a punch. Danny hadn't been in a fight since ninth grade, when he figured out how to get bigger guys to fight people for him. I looked at him, and the moment for apologies never came. He looked at me and said, "You're a fuckup."

He pushed his way through the crowd and outside. It was just as well. Maybe he was right, maybe I was a fuckup. I was going to pay for my beer and leave when I felt a hand on my elbow and a voice in my ear asking if she could buy me a drink. I said yes to the woman with honey-colored hair. She was wearing a business suit of navy blue and pearls.

Up close, she radiated the same type of physical confidence that athletes had. Only she was wearing perfume and it smelled good.

"What did you do to make your friend so mad at you?"

"I'm still trying to figure that out. I feel like he's been mad at me for years."

The drinks came. Apparently I wanted bourbon and she white wine. Who was I to argue? "No, seriously, he wants me to get a normal job, get married, have kids, and live in the suburbs. In his words, he wants me to grow up."

"You don't have a normal job?"

"Not normal enough for him." We made small talk for a while and had more drinks.

"You can't blame Danny, he's under a great deal of stress. Andy, he's hoping that you are his ticket out of it." By the time my mind recognized that I hadn't told her my name, much less Danny's, she was gesturing to her open purse. I saw the butt of a Smith & Wesson revolver and her open badge case. The badge was gold and federal, the ID photo was smudgy, but the FBI in blue letters left no doubts.

"I am Special Agent Brenda Watts. Danny is in trouble. His mob friends think he is on the cusp of something. They know he wants out and they don't want that. They are worried that whatever it is, it could buy him his freedom. These are the type of people who don't believe in attorney-client privilege.

"They kill people for less. People who know far less than Danny knows about their operations. We don't know what they think Danny has, but we know that they visit him daily. There are arguments, yelling matches, and one name keeps coming up. Can you guess whose it is?"

I was not in the mood for rhetorical questions from Feds, even pretty, athletic ones who smelled nice.

"Your name keeps coming up. Something about you is

bothering them. Something about you and Danny is bothering them. Let us help you, Andy. You and Danny. Help me convince Danny to come in and talk to us? We are the only ones who can help you. Who can help him. We can protect you." It had never occurred to me that Danny would want out, much less with my help. Not out. He wanted respectability. He wasn't the kid from Southie. He wanted a seat at the table with the Brahmans.

I thought that Danny enjoyed the perks, the life, and the cash. Nice cars, power, influence, who knows, broads and coke, too. Now there was a chink in his armor and his masters'. The Feds would drive a wedge in as deep and as wide as they could. The Feds were their own type of mafia. They didn't think they were because they were on a crusade for truth and justice.

"Agent Watts, what do you think I can do?"

"Danny Sullivan listens to you, trust you. If you helped us convince him to get out . . . to come to us."

"And give you everything he has on his clients? Ha. Even if it wasn't unethical Danny would never give up privileged information."

"He might if you were to help us. We might not be able to use all of it in a court of law, but think of how valuable that type of intelligence would be. He has a unique view into the world of organized crime in New England."

"Why are they mad at him?"

"They aren't comfortable with his relationship with you. You used to be a cop, you are a private eye now . . . not exactly their type. They think you are a bad influence on him." It was clever of her to put it on me. Give me an incentive to help, to want to help. They were slippery and manipulative, the Feds.

"You think you can help him? You are his salvation? I don't know what Wheaton and Vassar were turning out the year you graduated, but common sense was lacking."

"USC, and you and I know that he extends himself to look out for you. We can get him out."

"No, you can screw him over without my help. Thanks for the drink."

I left the drink on the bar, left Special Agent Brenda Watts, and walked out. I left her sitting there, looking good, looking like a dream. I left a pretty woman in a warm bar.

I walked back to my apartment in the darkening fall evening. Lights were on in apartments and old brownstones. People in the windows looked warm, cozy, and happy. People walked by in the street, heading home from work or off to meet someone. The occasional couple walked by, leisurely, arm in arm, more focused on each other than anything else. I walked, stewing in my anger and hurt. I walked along with the coppery taste of blood in my mouth. Danny was my oldest friend, and I had not expected any of this. I certainly hadn't expected the FBI. I wasn't sure what the Feds had, but Brenda Watts reaching out to me in a bar was not part of the playbook. The Feds like cases that are 100% locked up. They don't go in for reckless moves. I was sure they would keep coming at Danny but was reasonably confident that they didn't have much or Brenda Watts would never have bought me a drink. Maybe they wanted me to reach out to Danny, spook him, or maybe they wanted his masters to be spooked. Scare them into doing something stupid that would help Danny change his mind. That would certainly fit with how the Feds work. They wanted him, the whole enchilada to turn state's evidence. I couldn't see Danny doing it.

Or maybe they wanted me to jump in too deep. Danny would have to bail me out in their way of thinking. I couldn't make the plays, but then again, I was bad at chess because I couldn't see many moves ahead.

Why now? Why were the Feds interested in him, and why the big push right now? What had changed that they were willing to try to broach me in a bar. Something had changed. They thought he was in it for the money. That was funny, they misread Danny. He liked, loved the money, but he was in it because he liked not being one of the little people. The regular people. He wouldn't give that up for me no matter how much Special Agent Brenda Watts wanted him to.

Chapter 20

I made my way to my apartment and up the stairs. I turned on the lights and the radio. I listened to the news on the public radio station. I paced around. Pulled a book off of the bookshelf and then put it back. I went into the kitchen and looked in the icebox, but didn't like what I saw. I took out one of the green bottles of beer and opened it, but didn't take more than a sip. I lit, took two puffs, and then stubbed out half a dozen cigarettes.

The phone rang. The bell startled me, and when I picked it up I expected it to be Danny calling to apologize for being a grade A asshole. It wasn't. It was Shelly.

"Hi, Tomcat. Miss me?"

"Like a saucer of milk."

"Knowing you, it is a saucer filled with whiskey."

"Ha, too true."

"Tomcat, I am on the mainland. I came over for some shopping and now have a big, empty hotel room, with a big, empty bed. I could use some company."

"Where are you?" It occurred to me that I could use some company. That I could stand to have some of my wounds licked.

"Hyannis. Near the ferry."

"I can be there in an hour or a little more."

"Oh, Tomcat, you know just what to say to a girl."

We said our goodbyes. I promised to bring whiskey or grass. It would be whiskey. It also wasn't lost on me that Ruth Silvia's farm was nearby and that I could take a look at the fire. The timing of it was just too funny. That and someone had pushed me off of a bluff. And Danny had punched me. Things were getting weird.

It took me a little over an hour to get to the Anchor Inn. Every seaside town in the English-speaking world has an Anchor Inn—it is a law. It was evening and dark when I knocked on her door and she opened it. She looked great, big smile and mischief in her eyes.

"Hi, Tomcat. You are a sight for sore eyes."

"Normally I'm just a sight." She kissed me and pulled me into her room. My canvas mail bag ended up in a chair as did my coat, and I ended up in her arms. She pulled back and looked at the spot on my face where Danny had slugged me.

"Tomcat, what happened?" She was tracing her fingers along the slight swelling.

"My lawyer friend punched me."

"It seems like I can't leave you alone. Pushed off a bluff, punched in the face. You are not a very good tough guy." Well, she was right about that. "Well, Tomcat, at least you didn't say 'you should see the other guy.'"

"No, I never laid a hand on him." I said it with a laugh, but I was still smarting. I didn't have many friends left. She took my mind off of it by wrestling around on the bed with me. I let her win, but I was all right with it.

"Well, Tomcat, wanna see what this burgh has to offer for food?" She had wriggled into black boots with a little heel. She informed me she had just picked them up. We ended up eating at a small Italian restaurant, talking to each other about the things that new lovers talk about. Sharing stories of childhood and other intimacies. Her father had been an Air Force officer. He had flown cargo planes, and she grew up moving around the country and the world.

"How did you end up interested in art?"

"The post library at Pope Air Force base. They had these big books with glossy photos. Pictures of art that were beautiful. Fayetteville wasn't a cultural mecca in the sixties. I would take those books out as a little girl and pour over them. My dad eventually started to order them from special booksellers in New York and Boston. Then my mom would take me to art galleries. First in Raleigh and Charlotte, then Washington, then the Gardner in Boston, and then we would make weekends of it in New York. Paintings, they speak to me, the colors, the textures, the canvas, even the frames, the whole thing is a conversation."

"I had never thought of that. Not like that."

"Seriously. When I look at a painting, I see it very differently than you do. It isn't just a two-dimensional, colored picture to me, it is like a series of small building blocks that subtly add up, making a single experience." She was in love with it. You could tell by the way it engrossed her. When she was talking about art, she definitely did not see me.

We left the restaurant, deciding against a bar in favor of whiskey in her hotel room. We walked toward the Ghia, and the only other pedestrian nearby walked over to it and started to kick out the passenger side headlight, then systematically started to smash the heel of his steel toe work boot into the front body work. I couldn't believe some asshole was assaulting my Ghia, denting the shit out of it.

He turned to face us. He was big, thick shoulders and big hands. Longish dark hair and looked like he pounded nails for a living and just vandalized cars for fun. He smiled at me.

"How does it feel, asshole? This will teach you. I thought you would have learned at the lighthouse."

"What did my car ever do to you?"

"Huh?"

While he was puzzling over it, I snapped my left foot into his crotch. His legs started to buckle, and I stepped in and caught him from falling. Grabbing his shoulders for leverage, I twisted at the hip and drove my right knee into his crotch. He, predictably, doubled over, and I repeated the move into his floating ribs three times. There was no more fight left in him after that. I let him crash onto the cold sidewalk. I knelt down next to him and with my left hand grabbed a handful of dark hair.

"Listen to me, shit-bird. The next time you come for me, you had better kill me. If I see you, if you try this shit again, I won't beat you up. I won't hurt you. I will just fucking kill you. Do you understand?" Each word of the last two sentences was punctuated by a hard, right jab to his nose. He was retching but nodded.

I stood up. Shelly was looking at me the way the townspeople look at Frankenstein before they get the pitchforks and torches. She shook her head but didn't say much.

"Do you know him?"

"That's Troy, the ex I was telling you about."

"Oh."

"He's been following me around and calling all the time."

"Aha. Probably doesn't like that we've been spending time together."

We got in the car and drove back to the hotel in awkward silence. The rest of the night was a wash. We tried to make love, but neither of us felt much like it. She was freaked out by the violence. I was upset at letting her see it. In the morning, it was a little better. We had breakfast and didn't talk about her ex.

"What are you doing now, Tomcat? Going back to Boston?"

"Not just yet. I have to go check on a fire that might be suspicious."

"An arson investigation? Is it insurance fraud?" She seemed interested.

"Something along those lines." I didn't feel like explaining more.

"My ferry isn't until noon. I could go with you if you like?"

Eager for a chance to make up for the night before, eager to keep her interested, I agreed. The drive out to the Silvia place didn't seem as long this time. I wasn't drunk, and it was daytime. This time, I drove right up the long driveway, stopping the Ghia at the blackened ruin of her house. Just past the barn.

The barn hadn't fared well, either. The roof had caved in and the walls had given way also. The barn was a big pile of burned lumber and ashes. It looked as though it had blown up and the remains landed back on themselves in an uneven pile of burned lumber.

We got out. The first thing I noticed was the smell. House fires aren't like campfires or the fire in your fireplace. Those smell nice, folksy or woodsy. House fires smell acrid, burnt wood, burnt plastics, and rubber. Things burn in a house fire that should never be near a flame. Couches and carpet are little more than stored fossil fuels.

The roof had caved in, as had the walls. The foundation was just charred rubble. I was not surprised, given all of

the oil lamps she had in the place. Old wood burns fast—
it burns faster when there is lamp oil around.

"What do you think, Tomcat?" She was standing next
to me.

"It definitely burned fast, but I am not sure that it was
arson."

"It must have taken the fire department a long time to
get out here."

"Yes, they would have been in time to water down the
foundation."

We were walking around the wreckage. This is where
the TV detectives would find some clue that the arson in-
vestigators and the cops would have missed. In reality,
they were paid by the hour, took their time, and didn't
miss much. We were working our way around the back
side of the house. No clues, just broken glass from the heat
of the fire. No smell of gasoline or kerosene.

We were just coming back around by the front near the
barn when I heard an angry hummingbird whiz by my
head and then something smacked into the wood behind
me. You don't hear the gunshot first if it is coming at you.
You hear it whiz by, if it doesn't hit you.

I threw Shelly down onto the damp, muddy ground and
fell on top of her. The report of the rifle went off. It was
big, .30 caliber big, like an AK. She tried to get up, and I
pushed her down.

"Stay the fuck down. Someone is shooting at us," I
growled at her. I didn't like being shot at. I learned that in
Vietnam. I started to crawl back behind the part of the
building that offered more cover, dragging her with me.
Whoever was shooting fired four or five more quick
rounds. Then it was quiet.

Shelly started to get up, and I pulled her roughly down.

"Stay down."

"Tomcat, he's done shooting." Then the whiz, crack, crash of another shot.

"He was trying to draw us out. Wait for the sirens." I had the Colt out, but it was all but useless against someone hidden in the brush with a rifle. It didn't take much longer. Ten minutes and a lifetime of lying behind the burned-out house and then the sounds of sirens. They were heading up the main road.

While lying there, I saw something fluttering in the wreckage, something yellow, plastic. The only letters I could make out were TO on one line and then below it IPS. Potato chips. Why would the remnants of a bag be lodged in the joists? I knew an arsonist who loved potato chips. They burn fast and hot and tend to get overlooked because they are in almost every kitchen in America.

We got up slowly and then dashed to the Ghia. I drove back toward Hyannis with one eye in the rearview. We passed a State Police Ford and a Barnstable cop as they prowled looking for someone shooting a rifle. We drove to the ferry not saying much. Dampness, mud clung to my knees, and she was spattered with it also.

When we got to the ferry, I waited with her. We didn't have much to say to each other and we didn't hold hands. I walked her to the gangway, and Shelly started up it. Then she stopped and came back to kiss me. It was a short, hard kiss on the lips, the type that says goodbye.

"Tomcat . . ." She stopped, bought some time by brushing grass off of my back. "Tomcat, I don't know if . . . if you . . . Tomcat . . . you are a nice man . . . no. No, you aren't nice, but you are likable. I just don't think I am cut out for your sort of life." She kissed me, turned on her heel and walked up the gangway. She didn't look back. As I was walking away, I heard a familiar voice.

"Hey, man. Did you find the guy you were looking for?" It was the hippie, Ed Harriet.

"No, not yet."

"Oh, cool. You going back to the island?" His eyes were twinkling.

"No, I was just here seeing a friend off."

"Oh, cool man. I hope it was a real bang." He looked at me, holding my gaze for a second, and then said, "Good-bye, man." Then he turned and walked over to his truck, the green one with the wood. He started it and slowly drove it onto the ferry. I wondered if the hippie had a rifle in his truck.

I drove back to Boston. Did Harriet shoot at us and, if not, I wondered who had. I was certain that the fire at the Silvia place had been arson. But who, or why? Was it Shelly's ex taking potshots at us? We would have been hard to miss for anyone who knew what they were doing. Her ex didn't strike me as the sort who knew what he was doing. Neither did Harriet. As usual, I had more questions than answers.

The drive was uneventful. I got a crick in my neck from constantly watching the rearview mirror. Traffic was as good as it gets for Boston, and I made good time. I let myself into the apartment and started the process of trying to piece it together.

I called Danny and after a bit I got through to him. After I got done telling him what I had and why I thought we shouldn't pack it in just yet, the handset to my phone exploded in my ear.

"What the fuck is wrong with you? Are you fucking kidding me? What sort of shit is this? You not only don't find the guy, you piss off some broad's boyfriend, and you want me to keep the case open? No, fuck no."

"Danny, come on. Someone torched that house. Someone shot at me. Those aren't coincidences."

"You call yourself a detective. You found a piece of a potato chip bag at a fire. That is a pretty fucking far stretch to turn that into arson."

"Then who shot at us?"

"You were fucking someone else's girlfriend. I would shoot at you, too."

"Come on, man."

"No, Andy. You fucked up. You own it. For once in your life take some responsibility for your mistakes. Don't blame your dad, your mom, or Vietnam. You screwed this one up and now you are reaching, clutching at straws, so you don't have to feel bad. You fucked this up. No one else." He was yelling and he slammed the phone down. Danny was pissed. He wasn't the type to yell and slam phones down. He was so angry I never got the chance to tell him about the FBI's visit.

I paced around the apartment. I was not a good loser. I smoked or tried to. I didn't have patience for the pipe, and the cigarettes got crushed out quickly. I kept running through it in my head. Had I screwed up Danny's big shot at respectability? I took responsibility for stuff in my life. Blame Vietnam . . . what the fuck was that? Who the fuck was he to say that? I didn't use Vietnam as an excuse for anything.

I went around and around with it for a long time. I hadn't done anything wrong. Why should he be mad? I took the case he asked me to take. What the fuck did Vietnam have to do with anything? I stomped around the apartment, but that didn't help. I thought about what a dick Danny was being. That didn't help. Danny was under a lot of pressure to succeed, albeit self-imposed. But it wasn't like I hadn't tried to find the father for his client. I had tried; I had done the legwork. I had been pushed off the bluff, my car got beat up, and someone shot at me. I had tried, tried to fit in and get a job. Be like Danny and everyone else. Didn't he realize, it just hadn't worked?

Chapter 21

I spent two days brooding in the apartment. Two long days beating myself up and thinking I was a flake and a failure. Two days wondering if I had screwed up Danny that badly, and if what he said was true.

In the end, I decided to call Shelly. I was feeling low, and the last time I remembered feeling good about myself, it was with her. Her voice on the telephone seemed a lot better than going over Danny's accusations in my head. I went to the desk and began to rummage around for the gallery pamphlet with her number. Her number was on the back of the pamphlet where she had left it. I picked up the phone and held the handset between my ear and shoulder as I dialed. Listening to the clicks of the rotary wheel with each number and then waiting for the ring, I started to turn the pages of the pamphlet.

Shelly answered, and I didn't say anything. Not one word. I had wanted to talk to her. I needed to hear her voice—young, alive, teasing, and warm. Instead I couldn't talk. I wasn't even sure I could breathe. She started to say something about crank calls when I carefully placed the handset back in the cradle. I stared at the pamphlet and whistled. In the center of the trifold was a picture of Ed Harriet handing a large, vagina-like painting to a lady, apparently from the gallery. Ed Harriet, the nice burnt-out hippie. Ed Harriet, Charles Edgar Hammond, back from the dead. The caption read, "Ruth Silvia's nephew, Ed, loaning the Lightship Gallery some of her early paintings." There was more, more text about the show and more about the gallery. It didn't matter. It turns out that Charlie Hammond got comfortable. Got careless. Whatever he had been running away from, he let his guard down. He had his picture taken. He was the late Ruth Silvia's nephew. He had been there in 1968. Had he been there the other day shooting at us?

"Fuck me." It came out of my mouth slowly, and for a second, I thought someone else was in the room. "Fuuuuuck me." I had been right. I had figured it out. I had to prove it. Not to make it up to Danny or Deborah Swift . . . I had felt like I had lost. Lost faith in myself, and now I needed to prove it beyond any doubt.

I called Danny's service. I knew that he would be fighting traffic on his way home. I told them that they were to call him with a priority message. He would call them back and Danny would hear, "Mr. Roark said to rip up the bill and the final report. He has proof that the subject on Nantucket is the one the client is looking for. He will send definitive proof and final report in forty-eight hours."

I double-checked the ferry schedule. If I hurried, I could make the last ferry. I changed out of loafers and into jeans, work boots, and a shirt and sweater. I put on the Colt in its shoulder holster and grabbed my Bean's parka. A spare magazine made it into my pants pocket. I made my way to the Ghia and stopped only for gas. Traffic was thinning out, and I was able to make it out of the city in good time.

The ride to the Cape was uneventful, but my heart was pounding the whole way. The sky had gone from the early blue, inky hues to full dark. The Ghia was a dented Cyclops after Shelly's ex had put the boots to it, but it still got me there.

When I made it to the ferry, they told me there was no chance of taking my car over. There was no point in trying for standby. It was hunting season, and Nantucket was a prime spot for deer. Every year, hunters came from as far away as South Carolina to bag a Nantucket deer. The ferry lot was full. I was told where to find a private lot, which turned out to be someone's yard, where they were making a lot of cash by letting people park. I knocked on the door, but no one answered. I found an envelope in the Ghia, put a twenty-dollar bill in it—four days' worth of parking—and wrote a note, which I slipped through the mail slot. I made it onto the ferry with minutes, a few precious minutes, to spare.

I had no book and nothing to do except eat chili and drink bad coffee in the lounge on the top deck. The curtains had to stay closed, so when I wasn't eating or thinking about things, I would step out into the darkness and light a cigarette. I would smoke and listen to the throb of the engines and the hiss of the water parting under the bow of the ferry. I was crossing the water after my quarry. My hands shook slightly. I was angry for doubting myself and angry for giving Danny reason to doubt me.

I was on the deck with the wind whipping by and the salt spraying, and I realized I was looking forward to the meeting with Charlie Hammond/Ed Harriet. I was feeling the way I used to feel at the launch site in CCN, walking to the birds to infill. The gear had been checked and rechecked. Every man on the team knew their job and the other guys' jobs. Each man knew where we all kept the important gear. Everyone knew what they had to do and had complete faith in each other. The Americans and the Yards had complete faith in each other. You had to. The job was so fucking dangerous.

I had checked and rechecked my gear. The stuff I carried on my person at all times, the Silva compass around my neck. The Browning Hi-Power on my hip, hanging low like some jungle cowboy gunslinger. Pen flares in my cargo pocket near my laminated maps and a grease pencil. My web gear festooned with fragmentation grenades and spare magazines for my silenced K gun. The big white phosphorous grenade taped to my web gear on the opposite side from my upside-down knife.

There had been great comfort in the pre-combat inspections, the checking and rechecking of gear. It had all the familiar comfort of Catholic Mass. Then when you could check no more, you walked out of the briefing room, lifted your ruck, and fell in with the team. Yards and Americans, sun-browned and fit, moved to the birds. There were no white guys, no black guys, no Asians, just a team of men flying off to certain danger. Because the stakes were so high, there was a simplicity to it. You did your best. You trained hard. You tried to eliminate any potential mistakes. Mistakes, even the smallest of them, meant you were dead. You refined your game. Or an equally determined enemy killed you.

It was life distilled. Because it was so dangerous and certain, that made it simple. When I got home, life was chaos. Boston was chaos. The army, Nam, recon work all had rules. Boston was just a series of loud, narrow streets filled with more chaos and fewer rules. When I got home, I was shocked by the streetlights, stop lights, and short skirts. Cars moved impossibly fast by me and beeped loud, angry noises at each other. I remember getting back to my father's apartment before he died and just sitting there flushing the toilet. I was mesmerized. Except for R&R that I was too drunk to remember, I was in a real bathroom for the first time in almost two years. With a real flush toilet.

The shape of the island came into view, dark and low against the night sky. There were no stars or moon to be seen, but the red lights of the TV reception towers twinkled in the distance. Then the lights from an occasionally lit house. The jetties reached out like two welcoming arms made of rocks. Then Brant Point Light and the lights of the harbor. The ferry, named after that same island, slid into her berth, and I made my way down to the car deck. I recognized a trucker from the snack bar. He offered me a ride, and he took me halfway to where I was going. I told him I was going to the pizza place nearby. That got me halfway to the cranberry bog, where Ed Harriet lived and Charlie Hammond was waiting.

I walked toward the pizza place until he was out of sight and then started to put one foot in front of the other toward the rotary by the island paper. Then I headed down Milestone Road. By army standards, I didn't have far to go—four miles on the main road and another one down soft sand. For November, the night was warm, and the rain didn't start until I was half a mile in.

I remember night marches in North Carolina, in a place we called Pineland. Pineland was near Fort Bragg but a world away, meant to resemble Europe or Nam or the next place, the next war. Pineland was where you had your Green Beret final exam. You parachuted out of a C-130 into a piece of North Carolina that was best known for golf courses and national forests. You jumped into Pineland to help lead the resistance against some fictional Soviet-backed puppet. You were chased by members of the 82nd

Airborne Division, who were not hard to outsmart; they were just persistent, and there were more of them. They were paratroopers, meant to take the fight to the enemy, not chase guys through hot, humid woods. They were there because they were ordered to be there.

It was always hot and humid, like Vietnam—they wanted you to acclimate. After you linked up with the people playing the resistance and conducted your missions, the play war was over. You had to march out. It was always a lot farther than you were led to believe. No one told you how far or how much time you had. You just had to march, one foot in front of the other, and navigate without getting caught by some bored paratrooper. Then, if you weren't a fuckup, you graduated and went off to Vietnam.

Walking down Milestone Road in a rainstorm, I was back in Pineland. Headlights in the distance, and I would step off of the road into the bushes. Invisible to the people in cars driving on the only part of the island where you could drive forty-five mph. In Pineland, you had to carry a full rucksack, fifty-five pounds, straps cutting into your neck and shoulders. You carried a rifle, a heavy M14 with no sling. There were no slung rifles in Pineland. Your face and hands were blacked out just like in the old war movies. On Milestone Road, no one was actually looking for me, my face wasn't blacked out—I was just acting out of habit. The same habit that had kept me alive in the jungle. I didn't know why it was important to be invisible, I was just acting on some old instinct.

When I crossed Milestone Road and started down the soft sand road to the house in the cranberry bog, it was only raining harder. I was glad of the Bean's jacket and the work boots. I made my way down the road to his house, sweating under my sweater and jacket, without ever seeing a car.

The detached garage was still there, and the house was still there. I could smell wood smoke, and it suddenly occurred to me that I was going to have to knock on the door and say something. What do you say to a man who is trying, for whatever reason, to drop out from the world?

I trudged across the sodden yard, and as I got closer to the door that I wasn't sure how to knock on, it swung open. Framed in the light, holding a shotgun that looked very different from the double barrel he pointed at me last time, was Ed Harriet. This time he held an Ithaca 37, which was missing six inches of barrel and six inches of stock. A vicious weapon that you could empty faster than most by holding the trigger down and working the pump. I had seen Claymore mines that could do less damage. He looked at me, his eyes lit by the wild light of the lightning. I thought two things: one, he was going to kill me with the Ithaca. Two, I was staring at Charlie Hammond.

"The dog heard you or smelled you." He looked me up and down, a drowned rat and a mess of a man. "You'd better come in and have a drink." He turned away and turned back again, and said resignedly, "I knew you would come back. Just fucking knew it." He said it with just a trace of bitterness.

Chapter 22

I stepped in from the rain and stood opposite him. He held the Ithaca in one hand, pointing it at my stomach. He couldn't miss at that range. Actually, at this range, it would cut me in half. He bladed his body, still pointing the shotgun at me, and held out his left hand, palm to the ceiling. I eased the Colt out of its holster and watched him slide it into a back pocket. He turned and went down the hall to the kitchen.

He pointed with the shotgun to the same chair I sat in last time. He put two glasses on the table and a bottle of Old Crow next to them. He looked at me, sizing me up, and then put the shotgun in the corner next to him, leaning against the wall barrel up. "I trust I don't need that with you?"

"Nope, I am just here to talk." I was just glad not to have a sawed-off howitzer pointed at me.

He sat down and poured us each a slug of Old Crow into the kind of thick shot glasses you only see in bars. He lifted his and I lifted mine, and it burned all the way down to my stomach. I shivered, suddenly feeling the damp chill from my walk. He set us up again and said, "What brings you to my little house on a night like this?"

I looked at him. Now there were no traces of the aging hippie. "A long time ago, a little girl's father went out for a pack of smokes and never came back. She paid me to find him. She paid me to find you, Charlie Hammond."

He leaned back in his seat and said, "Ahhhh." He poured another Old Crow for each of us. "I haven't heard that name in a long, long time. You're a private eye?"

"Yes."

"And all of this is because I split a long time ago?"

"Yes."

He leaned back and his face seemed to soften, and he was Ed Harriet again. "Ha, aw shit. The dog freaked out with the storm, and then you showed up. No one comes around after nine on this island, much less walking up, sticking to the shadows. I didn't know what to think."

"What's with the sawed-off Ithaca? Are you expecting a whole lot of trouble?" Like a small army?

"Yes, I have been expecting trouble for ten years. Since you first showed up, I knew it was coming in one form or another."

"Look, your daughter is married. He is rich and about to go into politics. She hired me to find you to make sure that there were no scandals, or if there were, they could figure out ahead of time how to deal with them."

"And you? Do you work for one of those big companies?" He was looking at me across the tabletop.

"No, I am independent. Not even a secretary, just a dusty office in Boston." I didn't add that no one would miss me until the rent was late.

"Why should I help you?" He punctuated this by pouring us another belt of Old Crow, which by now was beginning to taste good.

"You wouldn't be helping me. You would be helping your daughter. I am just a messenger of sorts."

He sat back and contemplated this. "What do you need from me?"

"Can you fill in the blank spaces from when you left?"

"Sure, but it isn't easy. Do you mind if I smoke?"

"Not at all."

"No, I have some nice Thai stick. We could get stoned. It would be easier for me to talk about it." He was all hippie again.

"Sure, it is your house. Who am I to stop you?"

He got up, taking the Ithaca with him, and was back in a few minutes. He put the Ithaca back in its corner and put a pipe on the table. Unlike my briar, his was made of glass, like a giant, distorted marble. He packed it and lit it, inhaling deeply. He let out a breath of smoke and did it again. Then he held the pipe out to me. I hadn't smoked much since I got back from Nam. It had never suited me. I always felt paranoid, which is a bad thing.

"Hey, man, you want me to talk. You want my trust . . . smoke with me. Like the Indians, man, a peace pipe." Hippie Ed held it out. Who knows, maybe he had spent the last almost thirty years following the Dead on tour.

I took the pipe and inhaled deeply, and then again. I couldn't tell if it was good shit or not. At first, I couldn't tell if anything had happened. He poured me another whiskey, and I took it.

"Hey, man, you were in the service, right? I can tell— the gun is spotless and well-oiled, it is like a baby version of the GI 45."

"I was in the army."

"Yeah, I figured. If you were a Devil Dog I would have sensed it. Were you in Nam?"

"Yeah."

"Were you in the shit?" His tone was more than a little wry. "Did you kill people?" His voice had a funhouse quality as he said it. Or it was the Thai stick.

"Yeah." So deep in the shit that . . . he interrupted my train of thought, which was moving a little slower.

"I was in Korea. You probably know that. I was at the Chosin Reservoir, the Frozen Chosin, the Chosin Few. Yep." I nodded. He hadn't been in the shit, he'd been in the whole fucking sewer. He had been in one of the worst battles of the twentieth century, if not the worst.

"It was so fucking cold. We were hungry and cold, and I was fucking scared every fucking minute. The chinks would blow their fucking bugles, and you wondered if this was the last charge, if this would be the one that would get you. Each charge was like a giant wave, a human wave, a wave of chinks." He dragged on the pipe and passed it back to me. I was feeling, as they say, mellow.

"We kept shooting them and shooting them, and then they would stop. Then start up again. We were low on everything—bullets, food, grenades—everything except dead chinks. The only fucking thing you could smell was blood and shit. Not even that fucking kimchi, just blood and shit. It was too cold for the bodies to rot. That was a small fucking mercy." He paused to drink and smoke and set me up with both.

"I remember we threw away our carbines. They were fucking useless. They'd blow their fucking bugles, and it would start again. We'd mow them down with our BARs, Brownings, and our Garands, and we'd just fucking anni-hilate them, and we'd lose a few of ours, but we couldn't afford it, and they could. We ended up stacking up their chink bodies, because we didn't have anything else. Do you have any idea what it feels like to lean against a pile of dead, frozen chinks, hunched over your rifle, trying to make more?" The question was purely rhetorical.

"Dead fucking chinks, smelling of shit and piss and blood and chink smell. One night it got so cold that our weapons froze. The only thing that worked were our fucking .45s. We threw hand grenades at them and every third one would go off; those froze, too. We had .45s and E-tools and dead chinks everywhere. How the fuck was I supposed to come home and play house after that? Raise a kid. Go work in an office. I tried. Then one night we were talking about going out for dinner, and she wanted to go to a Chinese restaurant. I knew right then. I told her I had to get a pack of smokes, and that was it. No packing, no planning, no goodbye. I just drove the car until I got to LA and sold it for cash."

"You want me to tell your daughter you split because you didn't want to go out for Chinese food?"

"Isn't that enough? Doesn't she really want to know why I left?"

"There are still a lot of years in between that she is curious about."

"Let me ask you something?" I nodded in agreement. My head felt like it was made of cement, so I nodded slowly so as not to tip over. "When you came home from Nam, were you fucked up?" Hippie Ed was staring at my face, not Charlie Hammond and his dead chinks.

"Yeah, I was fucked up. Couldn't fit in, be like everyone else. Some days I couldn't go outside. I was afraid I'd kill some asshole for looking at me the wrong way or beeping their fucking car horn. I felt like I knew some sort of secret about how the world really was, and they didn't. Like I had the decoder ring to the secret code. I tried college, and that was worse. I didn't want to be in a fucking fraternity and didn't have any goals. I was just happy to be alive.

"I also missed Nam. Watching the fall of Saigon on TV, I cried. I fucking wept, not because I cared about their fucking government, but it meant there was no way I could go back to the only thing that I had been good at. It was the only place where everything made sense, had a reason, and where I had people I could trust. It was the only time in my life when I had brothers. It was the only place I belonged.

"I left college and tried the cops. It helped. It was like methadone instead of heroin. I couldn't make it in the cops, because they were sloppy and fucked up. It was like they were trying to get themselves killed. Carrying a .38 Smith and Wesson and telling people to stop beating their wives, or to stop partying, or to not drive like an asshole. By then, I was able to go out on my own. That is just what I did." I had thought about it a lot, but had never put it into words. I had never been able to say it to another human being before.

"You went to see the elephant."

"Yep."

He reached his hand across the table, and we shook. Then he got up and came back with more weed and whiskey.

"Does she have to know where I was and what I did?"

"Yeah, man, she does. I have to ask because she paid me, and I gave her my word."

"And you aren't the type of guy to walk away or tell her you didn't find me?"

"No. Would you be?"

"No, I guess not. Guess we got nothing better to do than drink more and smoke the peace pipe." That seemed all right to me. The wind was whipping outside, and the rain was lashing the windows. It was not a night to be outdoors. Not for me, Charlie Hammond, or W. C. Fields. Sitting at a table telling war stories and drinking and smoking seemed just fine.

"Tell me the rest. Tell me about how Charlie Hammond became Ed Harriet."

"How did you find me?"

"I followed the VA checks. I figured if you were to be found in LA, San Francisco, or Las Vegas, Pinkerton would have found you. But there were three checks that came to Hyannis, to Ruth Silvia's mailbox, in 1968. Ruth wouldn't tell me anything, but her land records led me here."

"But you left."

"You must have gotten comfortable. Complacent. I had an old flyer from an art gallery. In the middle was a picture of you handing over some of Ruth's paintings. Then I knew."

"And you came back."

"And I came back."

"Do you know she's dead?"

"I read it in the *Globe*."

"Did you do it?" He was looking at me with cold, hard eyes.

"No, *Globe* said it was an accident."

"No. Is that why you were in Hyannis?"

"Yeah, I wanted to see for myself. It looked hinky. I had to go see it. Did you shoot at me at the farm?" I was mildly curious, with my giant, heavy head and heavy hands.

"No, I am a marine. If I shot at you, do you think you would be here?" I nodded my head, which felt like a seesaw.

"No, it wasn't an accident. Someone killed her and burned her farm to the ground."

"Why? Why kill her? Did you kill her?"

"Naw, not me. Ruth worked with a lot of dealers over the years. She fucked over most of them at one time or another. If it wasn't that it was almost certainly someone cutting in on her turf. She was getting old.

"Let me tell you about after I left. I kicked around LA and sometimes San Francisco. I was drinking and flopping and trying to lay low. I hung out with beatniks and writers. That sort of crowd. When I needed money, I could make it as muscle for some guys I had known from the Corps. I had no problem hurting people, and I was good with a gun. After Korea, it didn't matter—right, wrong, hurting people—it was all academic. It was weird, my normal life was with the beatniks, and then I would slip away and do work. I was around people taking bennies and smoking grass. Cocaine was rare but not that rare, and I just stayed away from H. Back then H was forbidden by the guys I knew. H meant long prison sentences, and the old guys felt it wasn't worth the risk.

"I spent the better part of the fifties and early sixties between LA and San Francisco. My friends decided that H was okay. It was profitable and they were willing to do it, but they couldn't be connected to it officially. Along the way, I learned how to cook H and eventually, when it became big, LSD. It was an accident, really. No one went out of their way to teach me, I just picked it up. Then I started to make some of my own stuff, and I would move it on the side. I wasn't greedy or stupid. I made and sold just enough to put some money aside. I only worked with people I could trust.

"With the people I worked for, you couldn't skim money. You couldn't skim finished product. That would be a quick way to get killed. But if you were smart, you could skim just a little bit of the raw ingredients. It took a lot of discipline to do. Just a little bit at a time. It took more to sit on the money, to move it and hide it. I wasn't looking to get rich, just to have a little to retire on."

"How did you?"

"I would go to Vegas with a small stake. Nothing that would be out of the ordinary for a guy like me. I would play, lose a little, and cash out. Then I would go back to LA or San Francisco and put the cash in a safe deposit box. Or I would buy gold, silver, or diamonds. More safe deposit boxes. I had an AWOL bag that I kept cash in and a gun. Just in case I had to run quick.

"In the late sixties, my old friends asked me to work for them in Las Vegas. I was muscle, but my record didn't exist. I had stopped being Charlie Hammond and was now using another name. The problem with Las Vegas is that there are people watching everyone and everything, and they are everywhere. I knew it was a matter of time before I would get caught. I started to build an escape plan. That was going to cost even more.

"I found some shmuck from back East who was cleaned out. He thought he was saved. He was single and my age. He drank himself to death, and I buried him out in the desert. His identification and life became mine. I slowly built it up. Ed Harriet lived in Reno. He was a laborer. He had a car and rented a house. Ed Harriet paid bills and never broke any laws. Ed Harriet was a cutout that I stepped into one day."

"What happened?"

"It started to feel weird. Guys who I worked with were just a little standoffish. People were starting to look at me out of the corners of their eyes. It was only a matter of time before someone I thought was a friend would put a bullet in my head. In 1972, I was escorting this East Coast mob guy. I took him to a cat house, shot him up with dope, and took the money that he was carrying. I didn't want to hurt anybody. I found out later the money was from a big mob family back East. It was part of their stake in a casino.

"By then I had enough of it and just wanted a clean break. A new start. I took a Greyhound to Reno and left all of my papers in a trash can at the depot. Then Ed Harriet got in his nondescript Ford, drove to Lake Tahoe, and headed East."

"What were you doing here in 1968?"

"I knew even then that I needed a way out."

"You were setting this up?"

"Yep, Aunt Ruth loved it. She liked the acid I made for her and liked the money I sent her way when she cashed out gold for me. She liked selling the acid I made to her hippie friends."

"She was your partner?"

"Yeah, Aunt Ruth always said I was her favorite. Plus, it paid for the commune and shitty Georgia O'Keeffe rip-offs. Which led you to me."

I don't know how long we had been talking. His weed was strong, and we'd smoked and drank a lot. The rain had stopped and, for that matter, night had stopped. The kitchen windows showed the gray light of a foggy dawn. My head and limbs were heavy, but it had nothing to do with being tired. I looked up at him.

"Yep, you're fucked up. It is a special blend of mine. I call it: The Shit that Killed Elvis."

"What now?"

"Now we go for a walk on the bogs."

"A walk?"

"Yup, you are fucked. My old friends still want me dead. I don't want to be dead, and I don't want to run. You, on the other hand, are just the sort of guy that no one will miss. You also admit that you aren't the type to walk

away. I know there is no point offering you money. I've
seen your type before. Like some asshole captain who says
to hold the line but doesn't know why or care about the
cost. It isn't personal, man. I just don't want to die." He
stood up and picked up the shotgun.

"How come you aren't as fucked up as me?" In my ea-
gerness to prove myself right, it hadn't occurred to me that
he might be dangerous. Small mistakes get you killed.

"I have been smoking my own shit for years."

"Ahh."

"Come, soldier boy, time to go for a walk." He pointed
the sawed-off howitzer at me and motioned toward the
door. It took what felt like an hour to stand up, and each
foot weighed a ton—hard to lift, easy to put down. My
arms hung at my sides, and I couldn't open the kitchen
door. Hammond had to do it. He had no fear of turning
his back on me. When I tried to hit him, he was already
outside by the time I raised my hand. He never knew or
cared. I saw my Colt sticking out of the back pocket of his
faded, bell-bottom jeans. He turned and pointed the Ithaca
at me.

"Come on, gumshoe, you solved the case. You got your
guy. Now it is time to go." His smile wasn't pleasant. I
stepped slowly through the door into the yard. He was
going to do what the NVA had tried very, very hard to do
and failed. I had made it easy for him.

The ground under me was squishy. It had stopped raining sometime in the night, and it got cold. Not just chilly,
but the raw cold of November in New England. The tem-
perature wasn't much above freezing, and the damp air
made it seem colder. My Bean's parka was still in Harriet's kitchen, and I was wearing an empty shoulder holster over my sweater. My damp skin underneath it made
me shiver.

When the rain had stopped and the cloud cover had lifted, it had gotten colder. The ground was damp and comparatively warm. The result was a very thick fog that made it hard to see more than a few feet. My stoned brain tried very hard to tell me where I had seen fog like this before, but I was having a hard time concentrating on putting one foot in front of the other.

Hammond jabbed me in the back with the Ithaca howitzer. Idly, my mind cataloged that there was no finer close combat weapon than a sawed-off Ithaca. His first pull of the trigger would send nine .36 caliber pellets into me. Then he could pump it, emptying it in about a second and a half. My mind recalled that it held four in the tube and one in the breach. I hadn't heard him pump it, so I had to assume it was five rounds. Forty-five .36 caliber pellets in under two seconds. If you couldn't have a Claymore antipersonnel mine, a sawed-off Ithaca was the next best thing.

"Come, soldier boy—" another shove with the barrel— "time to crack the case." He was pushing me toward a break in the hedge that turned out to be a path. I stopped short when I heard gunfire in the distance. The low boom of a shotgun. "Easy, soldier boy, just a deer that didn't know enough to stay off the island, like you." It was the first day of hunting season on Nantucket, where people came from all over for the deer. Pretty soon it would sound like some sort of World War I battle.

Hammond pushed me again with the shotgun. That would hurt if I wasn't so stoned, I thought. We went farther down the trail. The hedgerows melted away; then we were on top of a paddy dike, falling away to water on both sides. It wasn't a paddy dike. It didn't smell like shit, and I wasn't in Nam. The mist here was coming off of the water. I must have been looking around.

"That's right, man. You will live on every Thanksgiving when people have cranberry sauce from a can or some kid has cranberry juice, a little bit of you will be a part of it." He was going to kill me and push me into the bog—even wicked stoned, I could figure that out.

"That doesn't actually give me a lot of comfort."

"Can't take the risk of someone telling someone and getting found. My old friends are probably still mad. They are like the church, they don't like transgression or desertion. They don't like it when you leave and take a lot of their money with them. The guys from the East Coast mob definitely won't forgive me for stealing from them." There were more shotgun blasts in the distance. There were other sounds, too.

Charlie Hammond was no jungle soldier, and he certainly would never have made it on the Ho Chi Minh Trail. At first, it was faint, but through the pot-induced haze and the fog, I picked out footsteps. They were parallel to us and moving fast. Charlie Hammond's life had depended on bugle calls and weapons that wouldn't freeze. Mine depended on not getting caught by NVA trail watchers and elite hunter units. Somewhere up ahead would be an intersecting dike. That was what they were trying to get to. That is where we were going to get ambushed. Whoever they were, they were more than happy that Charlie Hammond was talkative.

There were other noises, too. Flights of birds that suddenly didn't like the cranberry bogs. Clumsy, seemingly half-drunk hunters calling out to each other in the fog. The deep call of the foghorn on some other part of the island. The metallic sound of a bolt being locked back. Some people don't trust the safeties on open bolt submachine guns. They were the type where the bolt is held back and slams forward when the trigger is pulled. Not the type of thing a lot of guys want to run around with, so they wait to cock it.

Little mistakes will kill you. Someone else making a little mistake will save you. I dove for the water. It seemed to me that I was falling forever, minutes at least. I bounced off the side of the dike and fell into the ice-cold water that was standing in the bog. It hit me like an electric shock. I heard a horde of angry bees buzzing above me, the tubercular coughing of a silenced submachine gun, and the tinkling of brass landing on the dike. I heard the Ithaca go off and knew I wasn't hit.

I doubt Charlie Hammond heard any of it. When I half crawled, half floated back to his corpse, he had been stitched from crotch to head. His head had smashed open like a watermelon dropped on the pavement. The Ithaca hand howitzer was nowhere to be found. But when I rolled Charlie over, I found the Colt 1903 still in his back pocket.

I grabbed it and pushed the safety down with my thumb. I crouched and eased up on the dike. I followed the sounds of someone fumbling in pockets and then ramming home a magazine. The thick snout of the silencer on the .45 caliber Ingram poked through the fog. I saw a dim outline of a face and then emptied the Colt into it as fast as I could pull the trigger.

I fumbled my own reload, thankful for the magazine release on the heel of the gun. I wouldn't have to look for my magazine. Lying in front of me on the dike was a man dressed like a hunter. His face had half a dozen .32 caliber holes in it. I would never know where the other two rounds ended up. The ones that hit were neatly clustered around his cheekbone. His left eye was gone, and his nose would never look the same. He looked like he took some shotgun pellets to the face.

His weapon was an Ingram M10, a vicious .45 caliber submachine gun that could empty a thirty-round magazine with a touch of the trigger. It was compact until you screwed the bulbous, foot-long silencer on the front of it. It was a brutal, ugly, effective weapon for up-close work. Hollywood loved them. He didn't have a wallet, no ID. Just a couple extra magazines. He had my picture and a picture of young Charlie Hammond. He had been a professional.

It took me a few minutes to find the shell casings that didn't land in the bog. I found the Ithaca hand howitzer and ejected the spent shell onto the dike. The Ithaca went into the water. I rolled Charlie Hammond into the bog and pushed him under the cranberry vines. The Ingram and spare magazines followed.

I made my way back to the house. His dog greeted me familiarly. I was, by now, an old friend. I took the shot glass that I drank from and the pipe and put them in a brown paper shopping bag. I searched Harriet's house as thoroughly as I could. I found a couple of old pictures of Charlie Hammond's brief days as a father and family man. I found a leather key wallet with numbered safe deposit boxes on them. Next to it was an envelope with sheets of paper detailing the bank locations. There was an old Walther P38 9mm, spare magazine, and box of shells. I took that. Who knew who else was looking for Hammond? I wiped down any surface I touched in the house.

My Bean's parka went into the paper bag with everything I took from Harriet's house. I took his leather hat and a coat of his, which I put on. I took his car keys and cajoled his dog to go for a ride with me. I turned off the lights and closed the door, and I drove off in his distinctive truck with his dog. In the receding fog, it would look like Ed Harriet went into town.

Somewhere on Milestone Road, at forty-five miles per hour, the pipe and shot glass went out the window. I heard them smash and knew that traffic going to 'Sconset would finish the job. No glass, no fingerprints. No loops and whorls to say that I had been there. I nosed the truck into town, keeping my head down and trying not to be seen. I parked in the A&P parking lot in the far corner, near the gift shops and Captain Tobey's restaurant. I got out, taking the keys. I left the window rolled down enough that the dog would have plenty of air.

I walked toward the bandstand by Captain Tobey's and then turned down the alley behind it. I found a small mews in which to take off Ed Harriet's hat and coat and put on mine from Bean's. His stuff went into the paper bag. The bag went into a public trash can a couple of blocks away, and I went to the ferry.

The ride back was slow and uneventful. I was keyed up and kept wondering who was going to try to kill me next. When I got off of the boat, the Ghia was where I left her. I drove back to Boston the way I had before, back up Route 3. I had three hours between the ferry and the car to work it out. No one knew I was on Nantucket except Danny. No one knew that I had linked Ed Harriet and Charlie Hammond except Danny. Charlie Hammond, who had run out on the mob with a bunch of their money. Danny, who was a mob lawyer. Danny, who was owned by them. Or Danny, who was willing to trade my life to get in good with the Swifts. Or trade my life to keep his mob friends happy. As far as the bodies on the island, there was nothing to tie me to them. Who knows when they would be found and who would remember me, much less tie me to them?

With any luck, it would look like Ed Harriet had a dreadful hunting accident, killing a hunter from off island. The shotgun shell would have his fingerprints. It was near the body of a man who looked like he might have sustained a shotgun wound. Who knows what his body would look like when he was found. Harriet's car and dog would be found within walking distance of the ferry. The single shot glass on the table next to a bottle of Old Crow would look like a man who stopped to brace himself before he left forever.

Chapter 23

There was no one waiting to ambush me at my apartment. I took the fastest shower I had taken since basic training and dressed. Clothes went in my postman's bag, and I broke down the Colt .32 and gave it a quick cleaning. I reloaded the magazine and switched holsters and guns. I put the Walther and everything that went with it in the bag, along with the keys, photos, and letter. My Colt would go in a safe deposit box on my way out of town. I put a five-shot .38 Smith & Wesson Chiefs Special in the outer pocket of the Bean's coat. A couple of speed loaders in the left-hand pocket. I walked out and caught a Greyhound to Providence, Rhode Island, after the bank.

Providence is a fine old city if you like political corruption, crime, and the mob. It has one-way streets, old mills, and some beautiful architecture on Benefit Street. Brown University and Providence College vie for academic supremacy of the city. Brown is trying to buy the whole thing one house at a time. PC is all about Catholicism and basketball. I wasn't interested in any of it.

The bus station in Providence was made up of rounded

walls and orange plastic chairs. There were whores, junkies, and beggars inside for local color. You could buy newspapers, cigarettes, and gum. I bought a one-way ticket to Cleveland and walked out of the bus station.

I made my way a couple of blocks away to the train station. It was a building of yellow-brown brick and, where there was wood, it was dark brown. It was a beautiful building that was in desperate need of some attention. It dated back to the Civil War, and the soldiers from Rhode Island shipped from this station along with the guns and uniforms made in the nearby mills. I paid for my ticket to New York.

I spent the train ride wondering how to get out of this mess in one piece. Either Danny's old friends had sent the man with the Ingram, or Deborah Swift was a much more ruthless person than I gave her credit for. Either one had a vested interest in Charlie Hammond being and staying dead. Either one had a vested interest in wanting me to join him. With Charlie Hammond gone, I was the only thing linking the pieces together. Now I had to convince them that there was no percentage in wanting me to be the same.

Pennsylvania Station in New York was neither beautiful nor elegant. It was a testament to the atrocity called modern architecture. It was a series of dirty floors, escalators, glass, and granite. It had plenty of beggars, bums, junkies, and whores. Bored cops walked around twirling nightsticks, like angry, violent majorettes.

There are a lot of hotels in New York, but The Algonquin was the one I ended up in. I gave a name and a bullshit story about not having ID. The desk man took extra cash to not care. I spent two nights with yellow legal pads and then a portable typewriter. I didn't get to sit at the Round Table having cocktails with Mrs. Parker and her set. Nor did I get to enjoy the hand-drawn caricatures of famous writers. I spent a third day making copies, going to banks, and seeing lawyers. Two of Charlie Hammond's safe deposit boxes were in Manhattan. I emptied one of the cash and contents inside without counting it.

I called Deborah Swift's secretary, and after a pause I was told that I was a very lucky man, as she was at The Pierre hotel in New York. The Pierre is the last vestige of regal New York elegance. It looks over Central Park and offers the service and charm of a bygone era. There is no finer hotel in New York.

The switchboard rang me through to her room, and we agreed to meet. She suggested her hotel suite, and I suggested someplace less private. She suggested The Russian Tea Room, and I suggested the park at the UN. In the end, vodka and caviar won out.

The front desk arranged for me to get a haircut and my beard trimmed. I looked less like a hippie and a bit more respectable, like a high school English teacher. I took a cab to Brooks Brothers and let them outfit me in a decent but casual sport coat and slacks. They also provided a dark gray car coat, made of a type of wool that was so expensive as to be obscene.

Another cab took me to the legendary Paris Theodore's Seventrees Ltd. I explained what I was looking for, and the mad, dark-haired genius himself attended to me. A shoulder holster for the Walther and a spare magazine. He also gave me the name of a friend of a friend who had a machine shop in a part of town that tourists didn't go to. I thought about the extra trip but getting caught with a silencer was federal time. I thanked him and took another cab back to The Algonquin.

I showered and changed into my new clothes. I adjusted the P38, a heavy, double-action, German World War II–

era pistol. This one was in good shape, probably made early in the war. I chambered a round and lowered the hammer on the live round. I topped off the magazine, flipped off the safety, and holstered it. I loaded the two other magazines, and they went between my belt and waist on my left side. My new sport coat covered it all up nicely. My .38 went into the left-hand outer pocket of the car coat. I was ready for lunch or a shootout. I picked up a *New York Times* from the desk and took a cab to The Russian Tea Room.

I walked in with the *Times* folded under my arm. I told the captain whom I was meeting, and we stopped to check my coat. The captain then brought me to a red leather banquette that was far from the door and, seemingly, the other patrons. Sitting at a table across the room facing us was her driver. No livery, just a suit and a large gun under his left armpit. He had not been to Seventrees Ltd.

She held a hand out to be taken, without getting up. I sat down across from her on my end of the banquette. I put my folded *Times* down on the banquette next to me. "I hope you will forgive me asking Arthur to come in. You sounded a bit harried on the phone, and I was hoping to avoid any irrational behavior."

"Not at all. You are quite right, and it is prudent."

"Like carrying a revolver in a folded newspaper?"

"Exactly. It is my version of Arthur." She laughed, and despite the situation it occurred to me that Mr. Swift was a lucky man.

"Well, why are we here, Mr. Roark?" She was all Lauren Bacall.

"I have concluded your investigation. There have been some complications that I wanted to explain in person. Also, I have written my summary of events. I reached into my right pocket, and Arthur briefly tensed up until he saw the buff envelope. I handed it to her.

"You should read this now. It will save me from having to explain some of the nuances."

"That is fine. I took the liberty of ordering." She waved her hand at a waiter, who was circling like a helicopter. Serving dishes arrived with cracked ice holding caviar. Chilled Russian vodka in glass dishes with more cracked ice arrived; plates with toast, smoked fish, and hard-boiled eggs arrived. She looked at me and smiled. "It isn't poisoned, and I am not a femme fatale. *Nazdarovya.*" She drank a small glass of vodka in one gulp. I watched her throat move and wondered if I kissed her neck just under her jaw if Arthur would shoot me. It would probably be worth it. I followed suit with the vodka. I helped myself to food while she read, nibbling on toast and caviar.

Half the vodka was gone, and the fish and toast weren't doing much better. The caviar looked like a hill with a large divot in it when she looked up from my typed pages.

"I think I understand a bit of your paranoia." I nodded. "You didn't know if I sent that man in order to keep this a secret."

"Yes, now it seems a bit far-fetched, but at the time . . ."

"I didn't, but I cannot say that I am not relieved. I have to assume that my father's old cohorts in crime caught up with him, and the timing was unfortunate for you."

"If you didn't send anyone, then yes, that is what we should assume."

"Now, Mr. Roark, is the time when you should tell me that you have made copies of this and left them with your lawyer in case of your untimely death."

"It would seem, Mrs. Swift, that I don't have to."

"It would seem, Mr. Roark, that you and I read the same types of novels." She smiled, and I understood why Ulysses tried every day for ten years to get back home.

"There is more." I handed her the safe deposit keys

minus the one I had been at this morning, the papers that I found in Ed Harriet's house, and the pictures of young Charlie Hammond.

"These are keys to safe deposit boxes. I looked in two here and secured the contents of one as a bit of an insurance policy. If they are all similarly appointed, it could be used to defray campaign expenses, or be a slush fund that only you know about, or it could go to charity."

"And I can count on your discretion if I keep paying."

I laughed. That gets said to me and most private detectives in one form or another. "No, you hired me to do a job and it is done. I have been paid. I am not looking for anything else."

"One does have to wonder in this day and age."

"Not about me." She didn't seem to hear me. She was looking at the photos of Charlie Hammond.

"What happened to him? Why?"

"Mrs. Swift, he was involved in one of the bloodiest, most brutal battles in modern history. He had to endure hardships during it that are inconceivable to the average person. That changes a man. Leaves a mark. Maybe he left because he knew how much he had changed and didn't want his little girl to see him in that light. I know that if it was me, I wouldn't."

"Thank you, Mr. Roark. That was a kindness." There wasn't anything left to say. I left her alone with her thoughts and caught a train up to Boston. I spent the night at The Eliot Hotel, as Mr. D. H. Hellman. Cash can buy anonymity.

Chapter 24

The Eliot Hotel is a modest hotel in a nice area. It borrows a little class from the Harvard Club next door. It does everything it is supposed to in that it provides a bed and some discretion. The Eliot is that guy or girl you go home with when the bar closes. Just good enough.

The Ritz-Carlton hotel, on the other hand, is Boston's grand dame of hotels. She is elegant, majestically perched on most of a city block, facing the Public Garden and the Common. It has multiple, easily accessible entrances and exits. It makes it hard to watch and easy to slip in and out of. This weekend, the weekend before Thanksgiving, it was crowded because of the overflow from the Harvard/Yale football game. Two titans of academia and culture, neither of which could have beaten a decent high school team, turned this one weekend of football into a game more important than the Super Bowl, but only to those favoring blue and crimson.

I was dressed to fit in. Loafers, gray wool slacks, light blue shirt, red sweater, and blue sport coat with no tie. I had, as a concession to my profession, the trench coat that

Leslie had bought me. My hair was neatly trimmed, and all that remained of my scruffy beard was a neat mustache. I had Charlie Hammond's 9mm Walther under my arm, spare magazines, a .38 in my left trench coat pocket, and a large buck knife in my pants pocket.

I had been at the bar for an hour, nursing a scotch and soda. An hour before that, I was enjoying lunch in the Ritz Grille in the basement, and an hour before that I had strolled around like a leisurely tourist looking in shop windows. I hadn't been followed, and no one was watching the Ritz when I arrived early. Anyone looking for a scruffy detective would have only seen an upwardly mobile Ivy Leaguer with a sweet mustache.

Danny came in and looked around. I saw him in the bar's mirror between bottles of top-shelf liquor. The Ritz knew no other kind. All he would have seen is my back and neatly trimmed hair, just like any other Ivy Leaguer. He sat down, and a waiter floated by and took his order. I watched him in the bar mirror for fifteen minutes. He kept looking around the room.

I finished my own whiskey and with my raincoat over my arm, sat down opposite him.

"I'm sorry, I'm waiting . . ." He stopped and then it occurred to him. "Andy."

"Yep."

"You cut your hair."

"What, are we married?"

The waiter came by, and Danny held up two fingers in the universal signal for two more of the same.

"How long have you been waiting here?" He was anxious.

"Long enough to see the guys who were supposed to be looking for me go by without seeing what they wanted. Next time use better help."

"Andy, it isn't like that." He sounded aggrieved.

"Yes, actually, it is."

The waiter brought two scotches and put one down in front of me and one in front of Danny. He glided off with the precision of a German sports car.

"Danny, let's say for the sake of argument that my hand in my folded raincoat," which was sitting on my lap, "is wrapped around the butt of a .38 revolver. Let's also say that it is pointed at your stomach."

"Andy!" Aghast.

"Danny, after I left a message for you, a man with a silenced submachine gun came to kill me and Charlie Hammond. I was lucky, and I am still here. I don't think the timing was coincidental." Danny sucked in his breath. In all of our friendship, he had seen me angry, but he had never seen this side of me. The side that had come out of the jungle by the Ho Chi Minh Trail when many better men hadn't.

"It is funny, because that man with the submachine gun had two pictures. One was mine. Why would a man with a silenced submachine gun have my picture? Oh, and a picture of the man he killed?" It is a strange thing watching a man you have known your whole life deflate in front of you.

"Andy, you were never supposed to be hurt. You were never in any danger."

"Danny, don't be an ass. He was carrying an Ingram M10. The rate of fire is eleven hundred rounds a minute of .45 ACP. It is hardly a precision weapon. It sprays bullets and bucks around like something in a rodeo. It has a useless little nylon strap in front that doesn't help. I didn't get hit because I was lucky. Nothing else. Charlie Hammond wasn't so lucky. Also, your other clients might like you, but I am no one and nothing to them. For them, I am another loose end."

"Andy . . . it wasn't supposed to happen like this." He looked as miserable as I had ever seen him.

"How was it supposed to happen? You weren't supposed to betray me after years of friendship. After being the best man at your wedding and the only man your girls call uncle? Was it supposed to happen like that?" My voice had raised up a little.

"Andy, please, please believe me. When you took the case, I thought you were looking for a missing dad. I didn't know it was connected to them."

"Is that what all the fights with them in your office were about?"

"How do you know about that?"

"Oh, the FBI told me when they were trying to get me to give you up."

"FBI? Shit."

"Yep, the FBI. Hey, Danny, if no one wants to hurt me, then why the two clowns outside?"

"They weren't my idea. They said you were dangerous."

"Oh, Danny, you really do think you are the smartest man in every room you walk into. Don't you see, they want me dead. I am the only thing that can connect them to Hammond. Well, they were right about one thing: I am dangerous."

Danny looked queasy.

"Were you always looking for Hammond, or was it a coincidence?"

"They were always looking for him. If I had known they were looking for him, I would never have asked you to take the case. They were after Hammond. He stole money from one of my clients that they were going to invest in a Las Vegas casino. He stole ledgers, documents that the Feds would love. They don't have any interest in you.

"He could have sent a couple of very powerful men to jail for the rest of their lives. They have been looking for him for ten years. They wanted him more than Deborah Swift ever could.

"I didn't realize that was who you were looking for until you were already involved. By the time I put two and two together and figured out that you were looking for their guy, I didn't know how to stop you or tell you. I tried to stop them, but you can't reason with those people. I told them if anything happened to you, I would quit. They told me there is no quitting. They told me what they would do to my wife, my girls. Andy, what could I do? I swear it was just an unlucky incident. I couldn't hurt you. You are my oldest friend. Andy, come on . . . you can't think I would set you up to be killed. You are like a brother to me."

"I was your oldest friend. You betrayed me for some silver, nothing more. You are being naïve. You said yourself you can't reason with them. You had to know that they would send a hired killer. You knew that I would probably be killed. You had to make sure your masters got their man."

"Andy."

I finished the expensive scotch and took out a buff-colored envelope and handed it to Danny.

"Here are my case notes and summary. I have already given Mrs. Swift hers." I then explained the elaborate precautions I had taken in case something happened to me. "Danny, you also have to know that Hammond had a safe deposit box in New York. I was curious. You should tell your friends that he left a lot of very incriminating stuff in there. That is my insurance policy. Tell your masters that it is in everyone's best interest that I lead a long, long life. I have no interest in hurting anyone, and they can count on my discretion as long as I am alive. If they are worried, you can tell them that they hired me and that I always keep my clients' secrets. That is what they pay me to do."

"Andy . . ."

"Danny, you and I are done. Over. All the years of friendship . . . you sold them to your mob friends. All those Christmases, all those Easters with the girls. No more trips to bars; no more friendship. You sold it all and sold it cheap. If I see you again, I will remember how cheaply you tried to sell me and I will kill you." I brought my free hand flat down on the table; it was loud enough to make people look. Danny looked sick and scared; he had never seen the Andy Roark who had run down the Ho Chi Minh Trail toward death. My face was hot, but not from the burning trucks and exploding grenades.

"Andy . . ."

"Goodbye, Danny."

I stood up and walked out into the lobby of the Ritz. I slid the raincoat on and the .38 into my left pocket. I was now one friend poorer and a little sadder but wiser. I stepped outside into the Boston dusk and whatever was waiting for me.